A shock in the mail.

I opened my mail—several flyers advertising new texts on the science of DNA, genetic testing and crime-scene investigations...and one letter with no return address. I didn't recognize the handwriting. "Ms. Billie McNamara Quinn." How odd, I thought. I never used my middle name, which was actually my mother's maiden name.

I opened the letter. Inside was a simple, typewritten piece of paper with the words:

I KNOW WHAT HAPPENED TO HER

Then my heart stopped as something fluttered to my desk. A tiny scrap of fabric, lavender roses on it.

A piece of the dress my mother was wearing when she disappeared.

Dear Reader,

Once again, I am revisiting the eccentric and brilliant team of criminalists and legal eagles in a Billie Quinn case. The stakes were high in *Trace of Innocence,* but now they've escalated considerably. Billie has to confront the origins of her very existence—her parentage—as well as her mother's murder. In the meantime, the Justice Foundation seems to be falling apart, and Lewis LeBarge, her most trusted friend, may be lured away to Hollywood to host his own legal and criminal analysis show.

Like all Harlequin Bombshell novels, there's plenty of intensity and action, intellectual as well as physical. And never has DNA been more a part of the headlines than now. I've always been interested in how cold cases are solved. The Billie Quinn books were born out of what I would want to read myself.

So I hope you enjoy. Please feel free to write me care of my Web site, www.ericaorloff.com—I love hearing from my fans. And look for the next Billie Quinn case soon!

Erica Orloff

Erica
Orloff

Trace of Doubt

Published by Silhouette Books

America's Publisher of Contemporary Romance

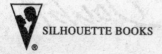

SILHOUETTE BOOKS

ISBN-13: 978-0-373-51417-5
ISBN-10: 0-373-51417-4

TRACE OF DOUBT

www.SilhouetteBombshell.com

Printed in U.S.A.

Books by Erica Orloff

Silhouette Bombshell

Urban Legend #8
Knockout #19
The Golden Girl #58
*Trace of Innocence #75
*Trace of Doubt #103

Red Dress Ink

Spanish Disco
Diary of a Blues Goddess
Mafia Chic
Divas Don't Fake It
Do They Wear High Heels in Heaven?

MIRA Books

The Roofer
Double Down (as Tess Hudson)
Invisible Girl (as Tess Hudson)

*A Billie Quinn Case

ERICA ORLOFF

is a native New Yorker who relocated to sunny south Florida after vowing to never again dig her car out of the snow. She loves playing poker—a Bombshell trait—and likes her martinis dry. Visit her Web site at www.ericaorloff.com.

To J.D.

Acknowledgment
As always, my sincere appreciation to
Margaret Marbury, my editor and friend.
Thank you also to Natashya Wilson, who steers the
Bombshell line with real vision and enthusiasm.

My agent, Jay Poynor, has never failed to support
all of my endeavors. And my greatest gratitude
to my family for understanding the ups and downs
and highs and lows of the writing life and deadlines.
A special nod to Kathy Johnson, who always reads my
books and never fails to cheer me on. As for the rest
of my pals—Writers' Cramp, Pammie and the usual
suspects—thanks from the bottom of my heart.

"No pay, shit conditions, I swear we're insane for doing this, Billie," he said in his New Orleans drawl.

"Insane?" I snapped. "This from a man with a collection of human brains in formaldehyde," I referred to my boss's penchant for the macabre as head of the state crime lab in Bloomsbury, New Jersey.

The two of us were making this particular field trip for the Justice Foundation, a nonprofit group dedicated to freeing wrongfully imprisoned men, through the use of DNA testing. Ever since we'd solved the Suicide King murders, the publicity meant the foundation was inundated with requests that we investigate the cases of hundreds of prisoners.

Deciding which cases to take wasn't easy. *All* of them said they were innocent. My guess is a fraction of them really were. We weeded through some of the ugliest crimes of humanity to try to discern which men were truly innocent, and we relied on DNA and old-fashioned detective work, interviewing and common sense to try to piece together reasonable doubt—or if we caught a break, proof of outright innocence. And all this we did on the side, in addition to our full-time jobs at the lab. What we had first signed on to do out of curiosity and Lewis's crush on one of the foundation's founders, we now did out of passion.

Marcus Hopkins was a baby-faced kid from the Bronx determined to get out of the projects. Unlike a lot of ghetto kids, he didn't pin his hopes on the NBA, or a rap contract, but on academics. When a rape occurred on the basketball court of the projects, Marcus was named as the rapist by the victim. No DNA tied him to the victim, and he had an airtight alibi—he was at work two bus lines away, sweeping out the supply room of a burger joint.

The crime was completely out of character for Marcus, and his public defender was confident at first. But then witnesses began piling up, placing him at the crime scene—despite what his employer said. Then his boss turned out to have a record—an old conviction for assault from fifteen years prior, but enough that a jury might discount his testimony in the hands of a tough prosecutor. Before long, the public defender was urging Marcus to take a plea. Marcus drew eight years in adult prison. With his pretty face, it was brutal.

We had a small spot of blood on the victim's

shirt. It wasn't hers, and it wasn't Marcus's, thus bolstering his claim of innocence. Lewis and I thought it belonged to whoever attacked her. She had put up a fight—and Marcus didn't have a scratch on him. But she had washed *before* reporting her crime—not uncommon in rape cases. A woman is usually so distraught, has such an urgent need to get all touches of her rapist off her, she may shower, in a traumatic state, literally scrubbing away evidence.

Lewis and I scanned the project buildings. Marcus claimed that there was no way the rape went down as the victim said because the basketball court had action on it 24/7. There wasn't any time, day or night, when a game wasn't going on—this was one of the city's top streetball talent courts.

"What do you think?" Lewis asked me.

"I think it would be awfully hard to rape a girl here, with all these supposed witnesses who just so happened to be too far away to help, but were close enough to get a look. Something's fishy here. And another thing, usually in the projects no one sees anything. It's like The Mob…you know? Everyone keeps his mouth shut."

I knew what I was talking about. My father was a key player in the Irish Mob in New Jersey. Bookmaking, loansharking…and whatever else he and my brother could get their sticky fingers on.

"I think we have to go back to our victim, Billie."

I nodded.

"I'm going to go take some digital pictures of the court from above, in one of the buildings, get a sense of what witnesses from the apartment may have seen. At night? My guess—nothing. You stay here. You'll be all right?"

"Or my name ain't Nancy Drew."

"Well, it isn't Nancy Drew. It's Wilhelmina," Lewis smirked at me.

Actually, my name isn't Wilhelmina. It's Billie, right there on my birth certificate, named after William Quinn, my grandfather, currently serving the last six months of a sentence on a racketeering charge.

Lewis walked toward the apartment building. I noticed, for the thousandth time in the half hour we'd been there, how the buildings blocked any wisp of breeze from blowing and cooling the steaming pavement. I was so hot that all I could think about was getting back to my apartment, stripping naked and lying in my air-conditioned bedroom on top of the covers.

The streetball game was getting pretty intense. A skin fouled a shirt pretty damn hard—elbowed him sharply enough I was sure he'd cracked his rib.

Suddenly the two guys were at it, big-time. Shoving, pushing, cursing and insulting each other's mothers. Their assorted pals were also getting into it, and this mosh pit of a group suddenly came careening toward me.

I sidestepped out of the way, and one of the players came and pushed me.

"Whatcha lookin' at?"

"Nothing." I stared him straight in the eye— well, I had to crane my head to do so, but I knew better than to let him know I was intimidated.

"You're not from here. What're you and that guy lookin' for, huh? Huh, bitch? You a cop?" He poked me in the chest.

"No. I'm a criminalist."

"What the fuck is that?" He was backing me up, pushing me toward the chain-link fence.

"I'm looking into the Marcus Hopkins case. Know him? He supposedly raped a girl on this basketball court."

In the time it took my eyes to blink, his hand throttled out to my throat. He wrapped his fingers around my neck—one hand almost encompassing it. I saw stars and my throat burned. My eyes teared. I struggled to make a sound, but nothing came out.

The shirts and skins were still brawling. If this guy strangled me to death, no one would stop him, and unlike the suspicious Marcus Hopkins case, I knew they'd all claim they saw nothing.

With all my might, I kicked my foot against his knee. He let go of my throat and started screaming, "Fuck!" I gasped at air as one of his pals came over.

"What's up, man?"

"Fucking bitch just kicked my knee!" He was leaning over, but he looked up and stared at me with total hatred.

I looked over my shoulder, hoping Lewis was on his way back. Then I steadied my stance in case I had to defend myself again. My face was wet with tears from when he'd choked me. "I'm not looking for trouble," I said.

"Listen," the guy who'd choked me said, "no need you go messin' around looking for who done that bitch. Marcus's time is almost up. Everybody's gotten their piece of the pie. If you know what's good for you, you'll butt the fuck out."

He stood, and with a half limp walked back onto the court, where the game was resuming.

I swallowed hard a few times. My throat ached. Time almost up. Sure. Five more years in hell.

A minute or two later, Lewis strolled toward me. When he got up close to me, he said, "What in God's name happened to you?"

"Don't ask," I whispered. "Not here." I motioned with my head, and we walked back through the straggly weeds toward the break in the chain-link fence, and then onto the sidewalk. My Cadillac—left to me by my uncle Sean when he drew a life sentence—sat by the curb.

I unlocked the doors, and we climbed in. I pulled out into traffic and away from the projects.

"Your neck is all red, and you have that whole Kathleen Turner raspy-voice thing going. We should get you to the emergency room."

"I'm fine," I said. He knew better than to argue with me.

"What happened?"

"I was warned off pursuing the Marcus Hopkins case. He thought I was a cop at first. Weird thing was he implied…a payoff. Something about everybody getting their piece of the pie."

"Do you know you have fingermarks imprinted on your neck? That's going to leave bruises."

I nodded. "You know this means we have to pursue this, right? Now we know for sure everything's not right with that case."

Lewis sighed. "I long for the days when life with you was normal."

I turned to look at him as I hit a red light. "Lewis…you knew from the first day we met— there's nothing normal about either one of us."

"I suppose not. All right, then, Marcus Hopkins—" he spoke to the air, to me, to the spirits he believed didn't rest until you put the real bad guy away "—I guess we're going to find a way to set you free."

Chapter 2

I reached across the bed at three in the morning and felt only cold sheets. Sitting up, I looked around through squinted eyes and saw the bluish light from the television set reflected underneath the door.

I bit my lip and climbed out of bed. The air-conditioning was on full blast, making it so I couldn't hear a thing but its drone. I pulled on my soft flannel robe, opened the bedroom door and padded out to the couch where David sat watching

CNN. He looked up at me and whispered, "I didn't mean to wake you, baby. Go back to bed."

Right after the Justice Foundation secured his unconditional release and he had become a free man, following nearly a decade in prison, he had been quiet but absorbed in his new life—eating his favorite foods again, being with loved ones, long walks with his dog, Bo, a saliva-sloppy Labrador-rottweiler mix who now slept at the foot of my bed most nights. David's prison pallor was replaced by a new healthiness. But C.C., the nun who founded the Justice Foundation with attorney Joe Franklin, said eventually the weight of what David had lost—ten of the most vital years of his life—would prey upon him. I saw that now. His deep-brown eyes were sunken, with dark hollows beneath them. He couldn't sleep, and when he did the nightmares often left him in a cold sweat and shaking.

I walked over to the couch and curled up next to him, snuggling against his arm. "You didn't wake me. I love watching television at three in the morning. Let's see if we can find a nice infomercial. I could use a set of Ginsu knives."

He smiled, despite his haunted look. "God, I

Chapter 1

You couldn't really call it a playground.

I gingerly stepped over used condoms, empty beer cans and wine bottles—the cheap stuff—and cigarette butts. I saw syringes and tattered underwear and the trash of human existence—fast-food wrappers, old tires and broken glass. Eventually I made it onto the basketball court. There was no net—just a rim bent off to the right. I looked up at the projects that surrounded this little concrete court of human misery.

Windows were broken, and the sounds of loud music and screaming and yelling in Spanish, English, Creole and Arabic drifted down. Smells wafted in the heat: Chinese food, the steamy air of the subways rising through grates, urine, gasoline.

"Charming," Lewis LeBarge said, surveying the landscape. "Remind me again why we're subjecting ourselves to this hellhole?"

We stood near the periphery of the court. A heated game was going on in full streetball fashion—hurled elbows and shoves that would have earned a foul in the NBA were just the way the game was played here. The shirts were playing the skins, with the skin team bare-chested, their tees wrapped around their heads to absorb the sweat from playing on an unseasonably hot June day.

"We're checking out Marcus Hopkins's story."

Lewis wiped at his brow. He wore his trademark clothes—black Levi's jeans, snakeskin boots that added an inch or so to his already lanky, six-foot, one-inch height, and a white oxford cloth shirt. I wore jeans and a fitted black T-shirt, with my long, black hair pulled into a high ponytail, and I was sweating, too.

love your sense of humor. You help me more than you'll ever know. But it's just hard, Billie. I feel paranoid sometimes. I try to make small talk with people at the library, at the gym, sort of get used to the world again. And I keep waiting for them to ask me something that'll reveal I was in prison. No matter how much reading and Internet surfing and everything I do, fact is I've been out of the mainstream for a long time. And I feel like everyone knows it. Like they can see it on me. Smell prison on me. And then I think about how I can't ever get that time back."

"I wish I knew how to make it better."

He leaned over and kissed my cheek, taking his forefinger and tracing it along the line of my cheekbone. "Most of the time, you're what does make it better. It's just the nights, you know? Christ, what am I saying? You do know."

I did. Some nights it was David who had the nightmare. Others, it was me. My mother was murdered when I was a little girl, and a strange mixture of memories of that night and half dreams haunted me. It was like walking into a fun-house maze and finding all my thoughts and recollections distorted somehow.

"Get your LSAT scores yet?" I asked.

"Not yet. But I really think I nailed the exam."

He had earned a college degree in prison, and with his conviction overturned and the real killer behind bars, David was free to pursue a law career. He intended to be a defense attorney and free other men railroaded or framed the way he was.

"You studied hard enough."

"Joe tutored me hard enough." He was referring to the Justice Foundation's lawyer, former NFL star turned legal eagle. David worked for the foundation now part-time, and the rest of his time was spent studying for law school or working on his book about his odyssey from prisoner to free man.

David caressed my neck. "I still can't believe that guy did this to you." My throat was mottled black and blue.

I waved my hand. "I'm a tough cookie."

He took my hand and kissed it. "That may be, but that doesn't mean I have to like what you do. I've been on the inside. I know how ugly it can be."

His tongue traced a path along my palm and then the inside of my wrist. I shuddered. Our physical connection was always high-intensity. I slid one leg over him and straddled him, and we kissed for a while. I liked to run my fingers through his thick hair, which curled at the nape of his neck.

"Tired?" I asked him.

"Yeah," he whispered. I slid back next to him and pulled the fleece blanket from the back of the couch over us. We sat on the couch like that, holding each other, for at least an hour, until we both dozed off. Next thing I knew, Bo was licking my bare feet and whimpering that he needed to be walked.

I stirred and looked at David. His face had a sculptured quality, with classical features. He rarely slept peacefully, but his face seemed serene as he slumbered, so I opted to walk the dog. I dressed in shorts and a T-shirt, took Bo for his walk, then came home and showered for Sunday brunch at Quinn's Pub. I dressed in a denim skirt and a black tank top, with an emerald-colored scarf around my neck to hide the bruises, left David sleeping and drove off in my Cadillac to collect Lewis and then go to my uncle's pub.

The first Sunday of every month is a sacred Quinn tradition. All Quinns not in prison are expected to attend, along with spouses, children and assorted stray friends and sidekicks we picked up along the way. Lewis was my usual brunch pal, just as I was his standard wedding date. David came when he wasn't cramming for the LSATs or, in this rarity, sleeping in.

I parked my car outside Lewis's house and let myself in with my key.

"Lewis?"

"Hunting for Ripper. Come on upstairs."

I rolled my eyes and climbed the narrow wooden staircase to the second floor. The top of Ripper's tank was moved to the side.

"How can a man who owns a pet tarantula lose said tarantula nearly every day? I mean, isn't this the kind of pet that you might—call me crazy—want to keep in its tank? Keep an eye on?"

"He's so gentle. I don't know. I take him out, I put him on my desk, we have a conversation, the phone rings or the teakettle whistles, or my e-mail chimes out 'You've got mail,' and I take my eyes off him or go downstairs for just five minutes, and next thing I know he's crept to the bathroom and is hanging out on my toothbrush. Just help me find him before we leave."

"Fine," I said. Then I sighed for effect. Lewis

really did try my patience. Just as, I'm sure, I tried his.

I began scouring Ripper's favorite haunts: behind Lewis's collection of brains in formaldehyde-filled mason jars; tucked in the eyeball socket of the human skeleton in the corner of the room, whom Lewis called Schmedrick; inside any one of the used but not yet washed coffee mugs that dotted the bookshelves. I remember once picking up what I thought was my coffee mug and finding the very large and very hairy Ripper nestled inside.

"Nope, Lewis, I don't see him anywhere."

"Here, Ripper…come out, come out wherever you are."

"Oh, Jesus! Look!" I pointed up at the poster of George Romero's *Dawn of the Dead*. Ripper was perched on the corner, looking as if he belonged to one of the zombies depicted in the poster.

Lewis nodded. "Ripper has great taste in movies." He walked over to Ripper and stuck out his hand. As if on command, Ripper extended a hairy leg and crawled onto Lewis's palm. Lewis then took him and set him down inside his tank, putting the tank lid on tightly, and placing a dictionary on top of the lid for good measure. He started to leave, then stopped, looked at the tank and added a thesaurus on top of the dictionary.

"That should keep the rascal. I should have named him Houdini."

"Come on," I snapped. "We'll be late for brunch."

"Don't want that," Lewis said. "I hear your brother's got a truckload of stolen DVDs he's looking to get rid of. I'm hoping he's got a few things I might actually want to watch, instead of like last time. I mean, who wants a DVD of *Showgirls?*"

"A lot of guys might like that."

"Please. You've seen one breast in a pastie, you've seen 'em all. Anyway, I'm praying this is a good haul—like movies still in the theaters."

Whereas I had long ago tired of the shenanigans of my brother and father, Lewis remained quite amused by them, perhaps because his own parents were so staid and boring.

Lewis and I descended the stairs and went outside to my car. I unlocked the doors, and we both climbed in.

"How's David?" he asked. "Sleeping any better?"

I shook my head. "Not really…. And you?"

He looked out the passenger-side window. "No. Not any better at all."

Lewis had an IQ over 160, and on a good night he usually slept about four hours, thriving on spending all night reading, playing chess over the Internet and often tormenting me with lengthy conversations about brain matter, blood spatter and serial killers. Then he fell in love with C.C.— a nun who for now was on a spiritual retreat trying to decide just what to do with her friendship with Lewis—and his insomniac life grew a lot worse, only now he was seriously depressed with a case of unrequited love.

"I'm sorry, Lewis."

"Not one word from her. Not even a letter. Or telegram. Carrier pigeon. Nothing," he wailed.

"She told you that she was going to go away and she wouldn't contact you. Me. Any of us. She was going to pray about this, Lewis, and she's just doing what she said she was going to do."

"But that leaves me no opportunity to talk her into marrying me.... And yes, I used the M word."

"I thought you were terrified of the M word."

"I'm more terrified of living without C.C. Do you know I've never so much as kissed her? And if something happened to me and I died before doing so, I might think my life here had been a waste."

"Lewis, when you're in love, you're more melodramatic than ever."

I headed toward Hoboken. We found a parking spot on the street and walked two blocks to Quinn's, already sweating in the pre-noon heat.

"Wish this God damn weather would break already," Lewis muttered.

"You're from New Orleans. Steamy humidity is in your blood."

"Maybe, but it's downright hellish around here. I expect this, south of the Mason-Dixon. But, my God, it's miserable in Jersey."

We reached the door to Quinn's, stepped inside and felt a blast of air-conditioning that was a welcome break from the outside temperature. My uncle Tony came over and hugged me, his bald head shining. He shook Lewis's hand and wrapped a tattooed arm around his neck. "Gang's all here," Uncle Tony growled.

Sitting at tables pulled together were my assorted cousins and my father and brother, and my brother's girlfriend, Marybeth.

"Hi, Daddy," I leaned over and kissed my

father. My brother stood and grabbed me in a sort of headlock.

"Mikey…" I snapped, "we're getting a little old for this."

"Never." He released my head and then hugged me tightly. "Got a whole truckload of bootleg DVDs in the back office there. Go pick through and take whatever you want."

I narrowed my eyes and gave him a dirty look.

"What?" he asked.

"Mikey," I said under my breath. "You promised me you'd straighten out."

"Come on, Billie…it's just a few DVDs."

"It's just a friggin' parole violation."

"I got the complete three-DVD set of *The God-father* trilogy. You love that."

I rolled my eyes but noticed Lewis was already heading back there.

"It's all fun and games until I'm visiting you on Sundays and admiring your orange jumpsuit," I said sarcastically.

"Come on, sit down and have a beer. You take life too seriously."

I took a seat by him and poured myself a mug of beer from the pitcher on the table. Sunday brunch was family style. The place was closed until four in the afternoon, so it was only family. My uncle Tony's short-order cook, Declan, right off the boat from Ireland—and as far as I knew with no immigration papers—made massive plates of scrambled eggs and home-fried potatoes, rashers of bacon and dozens of biscuits. Diets were forgotten in favor of good old-fashioned fatty food.

Lewis returned to the table with six DVDs—all horror movies, his and my favorite. "Nothing like some zombies," he said. "Mikey, good haul this time."

I glared at Lewis. "Stop encouraging him."

Lewis sat down, poured himself a bloody Mary, and a couple of minutes later the platters of food started arriving at the table. We all ate until we were too stuffed to move.

After eating, my cousins—I had over twenty first cousins on the Quinn side—all left to go to a Yankees game. They had offered me tickets a couple of weeks before but I hadn't been sure I could go, my Justice Foundation work was done in my spare time, which was precious. After my cousins left, my uncle Tony went into the stock room to take inventory, and my father, Lewis, Mikey and Marybeth remained, drinking beer and bloody Marys.

"I have something for you, Billie," my father said.

"What?"

He stood and went behind the bar and returned with a rather large cardboard box and a small black velvet jewelry box. He handed me the jewelry box first. "Open it."

I lifted the lid. Inside was nestled a diamond ring with an antique-looking platinum setting. I look at him, curious.

"It was your mother's. I know she would have wanted you to have it. It was our engagement ring."

My eyes involuntarily teared up. I took the ring out and showed it to Mikey. He swallowed hard a few times. "I don't remember it."

"Neither do I," I said, not that most children pay attention to jewelry when they are very small.

"Put it on," Marybeth urged.

I slipped it on to my finger. It was a tiny bit loose, but not so loose that it would fall off or I would lose it. I held my hand out. The diamond sparkled.

"It's beautiful, Dad."

He then opened the cardboard box and handed Mikey what looked like a big wad of newspapers. Mikey unwrapped whatever was inside the old newspapers—and found a statue of a bride and groom.

"That was on our wedding cake," my father said. He was still as handsome as the photos of them when they were young. He hadn't gained an ounce, and his eyes were still pale blue and striking, his hair black, with touches of gray now at the temples. His skin was unlined, except for the hints of crow's feet around his eyes and deep smile lines near his nose.

"Thanks, Dad," Mikey said. He turned the figurine over in his hands and then showed it to Marybeth.

Then my father handed me the cardboard box itself. I peered inside. "What are these?" I asked him.

"Cards and letters she kept—letters I sent. I guess letters from her mother and sister. Birthday cards. Valentine's Day. I couldn't stand the idea of reading them, so I stuck them in the box and forgot about them. You're the one who wants... you know...to figure it out. I thought you should have them."

My father never could bring himself to say, "Your mother was murdered." He always said she "passed away," conjuring images of a woman who went to bed one night and didn't wake up. And I was the one obsessed with solving her murder. I had files of evidence and theories. My very job was, on some level, chosen because it would enable me to learn more about her death.

"Dad?" I asked, "How come you never gave me these before?" I could only imagine what clues the box might yield.

He shrugged. "I don't know. I kind of thought it was disrespectful to…you know…invade her privacy like that."

I nodded.

"Why are you giving us all this stuff, Dad?" Mikey asked.

Dad sighed. "Well, with you two living on your own, I been thinkin' that maybe it's time I sold the house. I've got the condo in Florida and the place at the Jersey shore. Been thinking I might just get a condo around here. Don't need a big old house anymore."

"But…" I looked at him. I'd always imagined a someday when I would come home to the house

I grew up in with my own children. I mean, I wasn't anywhere close to having kids myself, but that didn't preclude the idea from being there. My childhood home had a treehouse in the big oak tree out back, and Mikey and I used to play catch out in the yard. Like every boy, he dreamed of the majors, until, unlike every boy, he started dreaming of hot-wiring cars. "The house?" I swallowed hard.

"I'm just rattling around in there. I mean, there's no sign on the front lawn yet, but I figured I better finally go through her things."

I held the box on my lap and nodded. We drank some more, watched the TV set over the bar. When Lewis and I were ready to leave, I kissed my dad goodbye and gave Mikey a hug. Lewis didn't say anything to me as we walked to where I had parked. When we got to my car, I unlocked it and put the box in the backseat. I climbed behind the wheel, and the first thing I noticed was the glint of the diamond in the sun as I gripped the wheel.

"You okay?" Lewis asked.

I nodded. "I think so. I just don't know why, after over two decades, my father has suddenly decided to deal with her murder."

"Maybe he finally needs some closure. Or maybe he can finally face looking through her things. You told me she was the love of his life."

"She was."

I looked over my shoulder at the box in the backseat. It felt sacred. I wondered, did that box of relics contain clues that would finally let me put her ghost to rest?

Chapter 3

That Friday at the lab, a television crew watched me analyze the tiny blood sample from the victim in the Marcus Hopkins case.

The crew was part of a news magazine following our investigation of the Hopkins case from start to finish—however it turned out. They filmed me looking through my microscope, and then they taped a mini interview in which I explained how a single blood sample was better than a fingerprint, and how it could unmistakably identify a killer.

When I lectured to college students on occasion, I liked to use the analogy of a bar code, and I used it again with the film crew. Every human being has a unique bar-coded label that is our DNA. The human bar code is different from a dolphin's. And my personal bar code is different from Lewis's, but it shares some properties with my brother's, just like all dresses in a department store have bar codes defining them as "clothing." But just as a BeBe dress is inherently different from a Dior gown, my bar code isn't exactly the same as my brother's, and it is completely unique, unless I happen to be an identical twin—which most of us are not.

After the film crew finished taping me, I went to visit Lewis, who was staring intently out the window of his office with an expression somewhere between angry and depressed.

"What's got you so glum?"

"I just got a call from Larry Harmon in the district attorney's office, who was calling after he got his ass reamed by the governor."

"And?" I sat down.

"And they want us to try to get through the backlog of rape kits. You've heard of Scottie Hastings. He's up for parole."

"Shit." Scottie Hastings was an acquaintance-rapist. However, he had a predilection for S&M that truly turned the women's ordeals into far beyond whatever their worst nightmares were. However, he was also very rich, heir to an immense private fortune—part of the Hastings candy empire. Plus, he had an IQ as high as Lewis's and read law books and texts on DNA evidence for fun. His dream team hired the most expensive jury analysts money could buy—and they were worth it. He got acquitted on nearly all counts in the only case that even made it past the grand jury. He was serving the end of a short sentence for sexual battery. No one had any doubt that as soon as he got out he would resume his sick hobbies.

"What does the D.A. want you to do?"

"Jailhouse informant says the guy brags he's got tapes. That he didn't only rape acquaintances. I guess raping people he knew got old. So he started raping and torturing strangers. Wore a mask. The D.A. is hoping he got sloppy somewhere and we can pin a rape on him. Preferably before he's out on the streets. The D.A. hopes there's a match in one of those kits."

"But the backlog is immense."

"Yeah, well, we just have to do it. I don't want this sick bastard out there."

I stared at Lewis. He rarely cursed, and the anger on his face was visible. "Okay..." I said slowly. "But something else is bothering you. I can tell."

He shrugged.

"Out with it."

"All right," he sighed. "Mitch Stern just offered me my own television show. A cold-case kind of program on their cable network. Five times the money I make here and probably a tenth of the aggravation. Says my appearances as a talking head are getting me network notice."

My mouth dropped open. "You wouldn't consider it, would you?"

When we were trying to secure David's release from prison, Lewis and Joe Franklin went on a number of legal analysis shows and cable programs to tout his innocence. Lewis on television was pretty much the same as Lewis in real life—dry humored, urbane, witty and at times mischievously ghoulish. He was also very telegenic, with his head of silvery hair and pale eyes, and that rascal-imp smile of his.

" 'Consider' is too strong a word."

"Oh, God," I felt myself panic a bit, "you are thinking about it, aren't you?" My voice was a little accusatory.

"Billie, every day someone at this lab is bitching about something—you being the lead bitch at times. We're underfunded, overworked and then we get calls like today asking us to do the impossible. Our testing is scrutinized more closely by the second because no D.A. or attorney wants to go to court and endure another OJ fiasco, and thanks to *CSI* and a half-dozen TV shows, everyone thinks he or she is a DNA expert, including juries. I'd be crazy *not* to think about it."

"But you're the driving force behind this lab." Lewis never lost his dedication to science.

He slumped in his chair. "I don't know what drives me anymore."

I thought about turning on my television and seeing Lewis, with Ripper on his desk, discussing maggots and blowflies with visiting experts, or maybe leading a roundtable discussion on how to dismember a body. What was the world coming to?

"Enough of my miserable existence. You read any of your mother's letters yet?"

I shook my head. "It feels creepy. I will, though."

"Want to grab some dinner tonight?"

"Can't. I've got to meet Joe and go over the Hopkins case with him. Want to join us?"

"Sure." He sighed.

"You know, Lewis, you're worse than a hound dog with those expressions. Unrequited love on you is ugly."

I stood and left his office, saying over my shoulder, "I'll let you know where and when for dinner when Joe calls me."

I walked back to my desk and answered e-mail. Then I called up the schedule to see where I could squeeze extra hours from the criminalists and technicians I supervised to process more rape kits.

About a half hour later, Ziggy came by with the mail. I'm not sure what Ziggy's real name is. It could be Ziggy, I suppose. I just know he's a major Bob Marley fan, and by attrition loves Ziggy Marley, too. At some point, with his dredlocks and faintly Caribbean accent, someone probably called him Ziggy and it stuck.

He handed me five or six pieces of mail.

"Thanks, Zig."

"When you gonna run away with me?"

"Zig, you know I have a boyfriend."

"Yeah. My dumb luck."

"Give me a break. Your girlfriend is stunning. She puts the rest of us females to shame."

"Yeah…and Shiana believes my band is just one break short of superstardom. She's a righteous lady."

"Yes, she is." Actually, I'd heard Ziggy's band, and Shiana was right. They were awesome.

Ziggy left, and I opened my mail—several flyers from a publishing company advertising new texts in the science of DNA, genetic testing and crime-scene investigations. Most of the textbooks were twice as thick as dictionaries and cost hundreds of dollars. Lewis used them to keep the lid on Ripper's tank.

Then there was one with no return address. I turned it over in my hand, then turned it back to the front. I didn't recognize the handwriting. "Ms. Billie McNamara Quinn." How odd, I thought. I never used my middle name—actually my mother's maiden name—because it was unwieldy, and people thought it was a married name and tended to hyphenate it.

I opened the letter. Inside was a simple, typewritten piece of paper with the words:

I KNOW WHAT HAPPENED TO HER

Then my heart stopped as something fluttered to my desk. A tiny scrap of fabric. Lavender roses on it. A piece of the dress my mother was wearing when she disappeared.

Chapter 4

"Jesus Christ!" I stifled a scream, then instinctively looked around as if the person who sent me the letter was there somehow, watching me, seeing how freaked out I was. But of course no one was there.

My hands shook, and I immediately put down the envelope and letter so that my fingerprints weren't all over it. I buzzed Lewis on the phone. We have Caller ID, so he knew it was me.

"Lewis LeBarge, resident genius speaking."

"I need you to come to my desk. This second."

"You all right?" His voice changed from playful to earnest.

"Just come," I managed to squeak.

Lewis was at my desk in under a minute. In that time, I'd donned rubbed gloves. I showed him the letter and the fabric.

"My mother's dress," I whispered.

"Are you sure, Billie?"

I nodded and looked up at him. I knew I had no color in my face. "You and I know serial killers don't retire. They may appear to stop killing, but they've either changed locations or MO, they're in prison somewhere on an unrelated charge. Or they're dead. All these years, Lewis, even as I've obsessed over this case, I told myself he'd met some gruesome end somewhere. It was how I slept—when I can sleep, that is. I told myself he was dead. And now…now I know he's not only alive, he knows who I am."

"Maybe a witness?" he offered hopefully, though I could hear how he didn't believe it himself.

"A witness who has a scrap of a murder victim's dress?"

"Could it be some elaborate hoax?"

I shook my head. "I don't see how. I'll need to have all this tested. The envelope, letter, the type and font, and the dress fabric itself."

"Whatever you need. You know that."

"Why now, Lewis? Whoever sent this, why now after all these years?"

"I don't know."

I got the evidence together and submitted it for processing, assigning it a lab number. About thirty minutes later Joe Franklin called.

"You want to meet at the sushi place in Ft. Lee?"

"Sure."

"What's the matter, Billie?"

"I'll tell you when I see you. Lewis is coming."

"Great. See you both around seven?"

"Fine."

I went through some more lab results. We processed everything from DNA samples to drug samples. If the police find a kilo of white powder, they need to be eventually be able to tell a jury if it's cocaine, heroin, or talcum powder. But I really couldn't concentrate.

My mother was the total antithesis of my father, but somehow what they had together worked. She kept a garden, read the classics, went to church every Sunday and she was from the old model of Carol Brady housewife—ever cheerful, running her household with enthusiasm. She was an amazing cook and absolutely breathtaking. My father said he was a goner the minute he laid eyes on her. At first, he didn't tell her what he did for a living…which was run a family within the Irish mob in Jersey. By the time he did sit down and tell her, she was already so in love, she made fragile peace with what he did even as she said a rosary each Sunday for his soul.

When she disappeared, the cops paid very little attention. They reasoned that she had tired of being married to the mob and had simply decided to take a hike. "Thousands of people walk away from their lives every year. They don't want to get found," was what one of the detectives told my father.

But her disappearance was so out of character, and even if she had tired of his involvement with "the life," my father knew—and always told us— that she never would have left Mikey and me behind. Ever.

And by the time the authorities took his claims seriously, the trail was cold. Her body turned up— what little remained of it—in a secluded wooded area six months later. Animals had consumed parts of her bones. There was evidence that she was tortured, some ligature marks worn into the bones that were there. And though it would have been convenient for the cops to dismiss it as a mob killing, the fact is the mob, while not a bunch of choirboys, has its own code. You don't touch the family of a mobster, no matter what he's done, and my dad hadn't been lying when he'd told the cops things were peaceful in his "business" at the time she disappeared.

My father was never the same after that. He wasn't home when it happened—and he told himself he should have been. I was never the same. Mikey was never the same. Her absence left this gaping hole in our lives. We were never at home. Dad couldn't cook much more than spaghetti or hot dogs, and if Mom haunted us, reminding us of the vacant empty spaces inside, we haunted diners. Breakfast, lunch and dinner, we ate out every day, usually at Greek diners, sliding across red leather seats into booths, plugging quarters into juke boxes on the table.

My brother followed Dad into the family business, but I tested off the IQ charts and was soon attending a snooty private school, with my father pushing me to go for it and become a doctor with my straight-A average and love of chemistry and biology. For me, science was about escape. And facts. I could write down a formula in black and white, and it was irrefutable. DNA fascinated me. And in that fascination was born an idea. I could become a criminalist…and maybe someday solve her murder.

Dad was disappointed. But I'm nearly through with my doctoral thesis, so I tell him that he'll have a Dr. Quinn in the family, anyway.

After most of the lab had gone home that evening, Lewis came to collect me.

"Why don't we go park your car at your place? You leave your car there, and I'll drive us to the restaurant. You can get good and drunk. I think you need to."

I was too drained to argue and nodded.

"Is David home? Why don't you call him and see if he'll join us?"

"No. He's drywalling his father's basement. Finishing off an area for his dad to do some woodworking." David's mother had died of cancer while he was in prison, but he and his father were exceedingly close. His father had never once given up hope that the real Suicide King killer would be found.

I followed Lewis to my place, then got in his car, and we took the New Jersey Turnpike and headed to Ft. Lee, a bedroom community for Manhattan just across the Hudson via the George Washington Bridge.

"Are you going to tell your father and Mike about the letter?"

"I have to. I just have to figure out how. You know how Dad gets."

Lewis smirked. "Yes, I do. Two words— Tommy Salami."

Tommy Salami was the overgrown steroid-huge pit bull of a bodyguard my father saddled me with when he was worried about me. When we were working the Suicide King case, Tommy had even taken a bullet for me. Which meant I was now forever indebted to a man who loved salami, as well as all other Italian cuts of meat. I often sent him gift baskets as a way of still trying to say thank you. But the last—and I mean the very last—thing I wanted to have happen was for my father to decide my mother's murderer was after me. If Dad thought I was in danger, I'd once again be riding to work with Tommy Salami in my passenger seat—I refused to let him drive.

"We'll have to call the police, too," Lewis said. "We can run the tests, but you know, tracking down the postmark and so on, we'll need to involve them."

I sighed.

"What?"

"Trust me. Finding anyone on the police force interested in solving my mother's case will be impossible. No man hours will be devoted to it. Nothing. Why? Because her last name, and mine, is the same as Dad's. And Mikey's. And their collective rap sheet is miles long. The Quinn name means they won't be looking to help us, Lewis."

"But it's a murder."

"An old murder. A cold case. You see how many rape kits we need to process. There are more pressing things for the police to do than find her killer. And to be honest, they botched it. When the trail was fresh, they should have looked more intensely for her. You know the department is loath to admit mistakes."

He pursed his lips. "What if I try to find a cop

to help us? I'm not director of the lab for nothing.
More than a few detectives owe me."

I shrugged. "You can try."

"Good. Because I was going to whether you
agreed or not."

I smiled to myself and looked out the window.
We arrived in Ft. Lee and spied the Japanese place
Joe loves, and then circled the block four times
until we found a spot.

We put change in the meter and entered the restaurant. Joe waved to us from the back. He's hard
to miss. He used to play football for the New
Orleans Saints. A bum knee meant he was side-
lined permanently, but they still had to pay out his
contract. Unlike a lot of guys who might blow
their proverbial wad on women and cars and
bling, Joe went to law school. His mother had
always wanted him to be a fancy lawyer anyway.
Soon, he was negotiating multimillion-dollar
deals for some of his old buddies, but a case he
took pro bono to free an innocent kid changed
him. Now he balances the big money with the
Justice Foundation.

Joe half rose from his seat and kissed my
cheek. "You look like you've seen a ghost."

"I have," I said.

Our favorite waiter, Huang, came over, and I ordered sake and Lewis ordered a ginger ale.

"Well?" Joe asked, using his chopsticks to pick up a piece of cucumber from one of the small spicy salads offered in sample-size dishes when customers sat down.

I told him about receiving the letter.

"You better be careful," he intoned. "You know, we nearly lost you on the Suicide King case. Have you thought about—"

"Don't say it," I snapped.

"I was just going to suggest Tommy Salami."

"I know. And I'm not interested in being babysat by Mr. Salami. I think I'll go to the firing range instead." I had, after the Suicide King case, gotten a carry-and-conceal permit. But I was still unsure as to whether I really wanted to carry a weapon.

Joe leaned back. He was dressed in one of his usual custom suits—you don't find clothes for an NFL physique in a standard department store. He had his shirts hand-tailored by a former Hong Kong shirtmaker, right down to the JRF embroidered on the cuff in elegant script. "This is getting tiring sometimes. Dealing with this shit."

"It's not the penthouse boardroom of some NFL team headquarters," I said. "It's the ugly and dirty side of life."

"Yeah. Well, I for one am tired of dealing with murderers and prisons. And I miss C.C." He looked at Lewis. "And not in the way you miss C.C. I just miss her calming presence. She was my anchor, man."

"How's Vanessa?" Lewis asked. He and I hated her. She and Joe started dating three months before. She was an entertainment reporter for a television tabloid show. She was stunning—and ambitious. And Vanessa clearly had no use for Lewis and me. The two of us wondered what Joe saw in her beyond her obvious beauty.

"She's after me to shut down the foundation and, swear to God, take a stab at politics."

I exchanged glances with Lewis. I could just see Vanessa taking over Gracie Mansion with Joe as mayor of New York City.

"You wouldn't do that, would you?" I found I was grateful for my hot sake, which had arrived, and I downed the first cup, then another.

"I won't say I haven't thought about it."

"What about Marcus Hopkins? What about men like him?" I asked Joe.

"I know. I haven't made any decisions yet, honest. I wish C.C. was here, though, to talk things over with." He paused. "You going to visit Marcus Sunday?"

I nodded. "I feel like I have to make the drive. David told me the worst thing in prison when you're innocent is the lack of hope. You just feel like it's a never-ending nightmare from which you can't wake up."

The three of us ordered sushi and spent the rest of the dinner discussing the Hopkins case, plus looking at files and applications of other possible cases to take on. I lost track of how much sake I drank. All I know is Lewis kept signaling for another one of those cute little sake bottles, and I kept filling my tiny ceramic cup. By the time dinner was over, I was definitely feeling less pain over the stress of getting the letter.

Lewis drove me to my apartment. Before I met David, I regularly crashed on Lewis's couch. Now I made sure I got home most nights. Before I climbed out, he took my hand in his.

"Be careful, Billie."

"I will."

"If it's your mother's killer, he wants to play some sort of game with you. Cat and mouse. And guess which part you're supposed to play? The mouse."

"Yeah, well, I've spent enough time with The Mob that I'm more like a very street-smart rat. You don't want to mess with a Jersey rat."

I exited the car and opened the door to my building and let myself in to my apartment. David was asleep in bed. I sometimes wondered if, after prison, with its inherent lack of privacy, he slept better when I wasn't in the bed next to him.

Bo came over to me and accepted a few pats. My cat slunk over and nudged his head against my knee. The two of them got along surprisingly well.

I flicked on the light in the kitchen and opened the fridge and poured myself a tall glass of apple juice. I was convinced hydration was the secret to avoiding a hangover. I opened a cabinet and took out three Advil. Hydration and over-the-counter pain relievers. I hoped I wouldn't hate the morning too much.

But they didn't have a pain reliever for what was really bothering me.

Lewis was considering leaving the lab for stardom on the boob tube.

Joe was considering shutting down the foundation for his ambitious girlfriend's career plans for him.

C.C. was still MIA.

My father was considering selling my childhood home.

My brother was again dabbling in the same sort of things that got him arrested before.

And my mother's killer had decided I would make a nice mouse.

No, there wasn't a pill big enough to fix what was wrong with my life.

Chapter 5

I trained my gun on the paper silhouette at the end of the firing range. Six shots later I had nailed my target square between the eyes, twice in the heart, once in the belly, once in the shoulder and once pretty close to where his family jewels might be.

I knew I was a good shot. What troubled me was knowing that if I ever came face-to-face with someone, conditions wouldn't be like the firing range, where I could concentrate and focus and aim ever so accurately. Guns were my father's and Mikey's territory, not mine. When I fired my handgun, I usually pictured myself coolly facing down my mother's killer, channeling my anguish into something powerful and calculatingly devastating.

I took off my ear muffs and safety glasses, put my gun in its holster and checked my watch. It was time to go home. David and I had made plans to take Bo to the park.

As I left the firing range, I thought about Marcus's case. And my mother's. DNA isn't done on every case. Now, more and more, it is, but there just isn't enough money—particularly if you have a public defender, like Marcus did. Sometimes, in old cases, tests weren't done simply because they didn't exist at the time, or because the advances in technology were too new. For instance, now we can test with smaller fragments of DNA than ten years ago. The specimen doesn't have to be as pure. The tiny drop of blood found in Marcus's case didn't belong to him or his victim. It opened a window for his possible release.

I walked the five blocks to my car. I had parked it down a side street. The neighborhood wasn't the best; it was a warehouse district, and Saturday left it abandoned. I instinctively shook my head to clear my mind and pay better attention. I walked taller and deliberately appeared more confident. I had been in plenty of seedy bars in tough parts of town with Dad and Mikey. If you don't look for trouble, but don't appear afraid, you're more likely to be left alone.

I reached my Caddy and started to climb in, but noticed a large brown envelope tucked under the windshield wiper blade on the passenger side. I walked around my car and retrieved it, opening it right away.

Then I screamed. Inside was a thick lock of human hair with what looked like dried bits of blood attached to it. I squinted and looked closer. The hair definitely had once been caked in blood. Someone had left me a "souvenir."

I scanned the street. I didn't see anyone, and it could have been left for me two hours before, when I first arrived at the shooting range. Then I got an eerie feeling. I couldn't identify it precisely, but a cold chill tingled at the back of my neck. I had the sense I was being watched. I told myself it was because I was unnerved by the sickening present left for me, but I wasn't so sure.

Hands shaking, I unlocked the car door on the passenger side and put the envelope on the seat. Then I took my gun from its holster and whirled around. No one was visible anywhere, but I spied an open bay on the warehouse to my left.

Quickly I dashed the few yards to the cement stairs leading up into the bay and climbed them to the open door. I went from the hot, blazing sunlight into the cavernous dark of an unlit warehouse. It was cooler, but also stuffy. I could smell old diesel fuel or gasoline, and could hear the scurrying of rats. Then I heard someone running in heavy boots or shoes.

"Who's there?" I shouted. With my gun drawn, I ran in the direction of the footfall. The further I followed, the darker the warehouse was.

Boxes were stacked high all around me. I stopped for a minute, straining to hear where the person was running to next, but all I could hear was my own heartbeat in my ears, my breath ragged and seemingly loud enough to echo. I was both terrified and determined to discover who had left me the package.

As I rounded one set of boxes, I glimpsed a guy in black pants and a black jacket running away. It was hot as hell, and my first thought was he must be a drug addict to be dressed in dark colors with long sleeves on a day with the temperature hitting ninety-two in the shade. Maybe he had the damp chills of withdrawal. I couldn't get a decent look at him in the darkness beyond figuring he was about five foot ten or eleven. I ran faster. A window was broken in the back of the warehouse, allowing light to come through a few cracks, almost like shards of sun. As I got a little closer to the person who'd obviously left me a souvenir, my heart pounded more wildly. He was wearing a mask. A creepy flesh-colored one that fit him like second skin, a Halloween-type mask.

I was instantly conscious of my gun. I tried to think clearly. *Fire the gun, Billie, and you had better be prepared to kill him.* To kill another human being. For what? Leaving me a weird package. I decided that retreating and calling the cops was a much smarter option.

I turned and did a complete about-face, running the other way now, keeping my gun at my side. I bumped against a tall stack of boxes, which teetered and fell over on top of me. The cardboard boxes, heavy with—according to their labels—electronics, smashed against me, knocking me to the hard cement warehouse floor. One hit my head, and I felt like I chipped a back tooth. My gun clattered to the floor next to me.

Panic started to overtake me. I shoved my arms out as hard as I could, pushing off the boxes, grabbing my gun and standing up. My assailant was nowhere to be seen.

I climbed out of the pile of boxes and ran for the bay door. Looking out, I didn't see him, but my eyes burned, and tears involuntarily formed from the sudden sting of bright sunlight. I leaped down and reached my car, opening my door with my left hand—shaking a bit, fumbling for the lock because I'm right-handed—one eye on the bay, aware of my gun in my right hand.

Gratefully I got the door open.

I hurriedly clambered in and shut the door, locked it, and put my gun on the seat next to me. I jammed the keys in the ignition, fighting the rising tide of panic, feeling like I was drowning in my own heartbeat.

Thank God, my Caddy is a dream. Her engine raced, and I pulled away from the curb with a screech of my tires. Looking in my rearview mirror, I saw him emerge from the warehouse, his masked face, almost like a burn victim's, expressionless and waxy. His hair, I saw, was a cheap wig. I gunned the car and as I picked up speed, I looked again in my rearview mirror, but he was gone, almost as if it had been some weird nightmare. As if it had never really happened. I didn't even dial the cops. They'd think it was some weird attempt to scare me. A stalker. I drove, pedal nearly to the floor, until I was ten or fifteen blocks away. Then I followed signs for the Turnpike. When I reached the highway, I pulled into the first rest stop. Only when I was parked and feeling safe, did I allow my sheer terror to bubble to the surface. My hands shook, my teeth chattered, and I wanted to scream aloud. I gripped my sides and rocked back against my seat until I felt the horror of that creep subside. Then I tried to think.

Was he the man who murdered my mother?

Or did he have something to do with a case?

Either way, I decided from now on, I was going to be armed. And I had a sneaking suspicion Tommy Salami was going to be visiting me very soon. Lewis was my best friend, and if I told him what happened, I knew he'd tell my Dad. It was the only time he ever betrayed a confidence: if he felt I was in danger. And for only the second time in my life, I had to agree. I really and truly was.

Chapter 6

In the predawn hours of Sunday morning, Bo leaped on the bed and licked David's face to beg him to go out. David groaned but rose and slipped into shorts to take him. I rolled over and snuggled deeper under the covers, where I felt safe.

About fifteen minutes later David returned, dropped his shorts to the floor and slid back into bed with me. He spooned around me, his body like a perfect sculpture, like the statue of David. "I love you, Billie."

"Love you, too," I murmured.

"I really wish you'd call the police." He kissed the nape of my neck and with tiny flicks of his tongue, kissed all the way to my shoulder, which was bruised from my fall in the warehouse.

"No." After my attack, I had driven to the lab to have the souvenir in the envelope processed. "I think it has to do with my mother's case. And they didn't help my family before, so it's not like I want their help now. You, more than anyone, should understand that."

When David was arrested, he had an iffy alibi but impeccable character witnesses—and no visible motive. But the police seemed only too happy to consider the case closed. Of course, it turned out one of the men in blue had done it.

He kissed my bare shoulder. "I do."

We lay there in silence for a while. Sometimes, David and I were like two islands, separated by the choppy waters of the tragedies that had happened to each of us. Sometimes we clung to each other desperately, like two survivors of a shipwreck.

The sun came up, and I rose and made a pot of coffee. I fed my cat and then showered and got ready for the long ride to see Marcus.

This particular Sunday I liked the quiet of the four-hour or so drive to Dannemora, which rises like a fortress in upstate New York. My family, anyone who's spent time there, calls it Little Siberia. In the winter, Oneida County might as well be the real Siberia. Snowfall is measured in *feet,* not inches. The lake system means lots of white-outs, snow and fog blowing in off the water. It's desolate and despairing. And in the midst of this harsh landscape, the stone prison rises, forbidding, like an evil queen's torturous snow palace.

In contrast, during the summer, the area around Dannemora is green and lush. But it's still isolated. No one else lives in Clinton, New York, except the prison guards, workers and their families. I mean, others do, but the town mostly exists for the support of Little Siberia.

I've spent much of my life visiting relatives in prison, including my grandfather. Each penitentiary has its own atmosphere and variations on the rules. My father and Mikey usually served at minimum-security facilities. I had uncles who served in Dannemora, Sing-Sing and Auburn. One of my more troubled cousins even got involved in a major drug-trafficking scheme and is serving in the escape-proof federal facility in Leavenworth, Kansas. He'll be there a long time, thanks to minimum-sentencing guidelines. He's gone practically mad from the lack of human contact there—his behavior's earned him time in a lockdown section where no natural light ever makes its way in.

Prison has sounds like no other place. An echoing roar of male voices, almost like a buzzing hive of killer bees. Bars clanging, buzzers sounding, shouts, screams, catcalls, whistles, televisions blaring. If you watch carefully, you can see men communicating with hand signals. Gang signs flash. When I arrived at Dannemora, I waited to be processed, identified as one of Marcus Hopkins's defense-team members. Eventually I was shown to a meeting room where Marcus and I could talk.

Guards in dark-blue uniforms brought him in. Marcus sat down and flashed me a half smile. He had two deep-set dimples and was still boyish despite packing on forty pounds of muscle in the prison yard over the years. In a world where justice worked perfectly, he would have been off at college, flashing that smile at girls, and spending his days in the library. His IQ was 139. He had a lock on a scholarship out of the projects until he was railroaded.

"Hi, Marcus." I smiled back at him. I was a poor substitute for C.C., who had made prison ministry her life. I couldn't quote the Bible or Camus or Sartre, or Buddha or Thich Nhat Hanh, or any of the thousands of wise words and quotations she had for these men. I knew she combed Emerson, C. S. Lewis, and the Bible for bits of hope. A phrase to hold on to when the nights were dark and the days seemed darker. I had only a passing acquaintance with God. C.C. and God, on the other hand, were on a first-name basis.

"Anything new on my case?"

"We went to the basketball court to retrace the crime. We tested the drop of blood—not a match for you or Kenora. So that's something. We're tracking her down to interview her. She left the projects. Any idea where she might have gone? You hear anything?"

He shrugged. "My grandmother died. Don't have anybody living there anymore."

"We'll find her. You doing okay in here?" I internally berated myself. What was he supposed to say?

"Drives me crazy not being free. When I get out of here, it's going to take me a long, long time to wash the stench of prison off me. I sometimes picture it. Taking a shower with near-boiling water and scrubbing my skin until it's raw and bloody. But I still don't know if that will do the trick."

I thought of David. I could see the times he was far away from me. Back in prison—in his mind. Sometimes, I came home when he was in the middle of doing his sit-ups and push-ups. He could do five hundred of each without blinking. While he was doing them, his face was intense, stoic, as if he was in his cell doing them in a fury for the injustice done to him.

"Marcus." I squinted at him. He was bouncing his leg up and down as he talked, fidgeting. "You nervous about something?"

He nodded and looked down at the table. Then he looked up at me. "I was in the library. Looking up some stuff pertinent to my case. Just reading up in some law books. Got to talking to another guy in there. Mentioned the foundation taking on my case."

He fidgeted with his fingers. "Next day, I'm in the yard. I ended up being asked to go sit with some white guy who kind of runs The Mob boys."

I was familiar with the way the yard worked. Mob boys—Italians. Mob boys—Irish. Black guys. Black Muslim guys. Gang bangers divided by gang. Mexicans. Mexicans who identified themselves as Chicano. Prison was really a microcosm for how most of the world worked. Everyone stayed with their own kind. Land of the free, home of the brave, but most people wouldn't break bread with someone from another race in their day-to-day lives.

"Okay. What did he want?" I presumed it was for us to take his case, too. And I thought it would be a very hot day in January in Little Siberia before I got involved defending The Mob.

"His name's Marty O'Hare. And he wanted me to give you a message. Says to tell you he's your old man's rival, and everyone knows your old man isn't your old man."

"What the hell is that supposed to mean?"

"Means, Billie, that Marty says your mother was having an affair when she died. And your father isn't really your father."

The already-close, drab walls of our meeting room started feeling closer.

"What is he talking about?"

"He said to look into it."

"I'm not in the mood for another wild-goose chase. Who does this asshole think he is?"

"Billie," Marcus held up his hands. "Don't shoot the messenger. I didn't even want to deliver the message. But they said they'd watch my back a little if I did."

I blushed, feeling ashamed at lashing out at him. "I'm sorry, Marcus. I didn't mean to give you a hard time. I just don't understand."

He shrugged. The two of us chatted for a while. Then my visiting time was up. When C.C. left on her retreat, I swore to her I would visit "our boys"—the cases we took on. I rotated who I visited and tried to see one or two a month to offer hope, offer contact, to let them know the world had not forgotten them.

"You know you can call collect anytime," I said as I bid him goodbye. It always hurt to leave him there, believing in my heart he was innocent. I remembered leaving David in prison and driving away, feeling a steady ache in my chest. Sometimes, and I never even told Lewis this, I used to cry when I left David. I never knew how C.C. did it. All those lost men, falsely imprisoned.

But she got her strength from something far greater than herself.

I got back in my car and settled in for the long ride home. It would be well after dark by the time I got there, but I was grateful for the drive. It gave me a chance to go over things in my mind before I had to deal with Lewis—or my Dad. I turned the dial to a jazz station—music without words that would let me turn over things in my head.

I had assumed my mom was murdered by a serial killer. Was it possible that all this time it was a personal murder?

Statistically people are killed by those closest to them. It's personal. It's vengeful. It's that moment someone snaps. Or it's that cold, calculating moment when a man decides he doesn't want to pay out child support for the rest of his life and he strangles his pregnant wife to death. That's what got Scott Peterson. He was a cold-blooded murderer, and he was having an affair, and the minute those cops took the call, they knew. They may have kept an open mind, but they knew. The stats were on their side. And if they were patient long enough, they'd nail him. And they did.

I hadn't thought, in all these years, that my

mother had been anything but what I saw. I had never asked my aunt if my mother had been having an affair. If it was true, I didn't hate her. She was human. No one was perfect. But I would be upset with myself for neglecting the obvious. I guess it had seemed disrespectful to my parents' marriage to even think about it.

I swallowed hard as I drove down the New York Thruway. Upstate, it's so clear and perfect. I passed by lakes and signs for cabins. A person could chop up a body and bury it up here and no one would ever find it. That's what my work made me think. Not *What lovely scenery.* No, I thought, *Wonder how fast the maggots would invade up here.*

I shook my head, and my thoughts shifted back to my parents. Does every child believe in the fairy tale of their parents' love until divorce or some other dirty secret? I firmly believed they were the loves of each other's lives. But maybe the police weren't totally wrong. Maybe she had tired of the life. Maybe one too many calls at 3:00 a.m. to bring bail money, or one too many times that he came home with a bag of cash that she couldn't ask any questions about.

I knew the O'Hare name. He and my father had

been rivals, until Marty got caught in a major sting having to do with fake lottery scratch-offs. When cornered, Marty opened fire on the cops—thus earning him a nice, long stretch in Little Siberia. Was this just Marty's way of exacting a little revenge on Dad? Or was it true? Did my mother's lover have something to do with her disappearance? Could it be that after spending my entire life with the Quinns, the rowdy, rough but ultimately loyal clan, that I wasn't really a Quinn at all?

Chapter 7

I arrived back at my apartment around ten that night. Ordinarily I don't think much of walking from my car to my apartment, but since the warehouse, since the letter from my mother's killer, everything had changed.

I let myself in. David and Bo weren't there. Sometimes David stayed at his dad's. I was grateful he wasn't home because my head was swimming—too many diverging theories and possibilities were suddenly appearing in my mother's case. The trail had been so cold it was icy—and yet now, all of a sudden, it was hot again.

I went to the kitchen and pulled down a wine-glass and poured myself a pinot noir. My brother had gifted me a case of a nice Australian vintage—stolen, I'm sure. I learned long ago not to look a gift horse in the mouth with my brother and father. I learned not to look for gift receipts, either. I just smiled and accepted that their hearts were in the right place.

Taking my wine, I went to the bedroom, turned on the light, opened the closet door, and pulled down the box of cards and keepsakes my father had given me.

Sitting down on the bed, I lifted the lid, smelling the musty scent of the attic where he'd kept the box for so long. Pulling out a stack of cards, I started opening them. Most were the Valentine's cards Dad had sent her. All of them had handwritten notes. It was a side of my dad lost forever when she died:

To My Darling,
Every day I'm grateful you are in my life. If I hadn't met you, I don't think anything in

my life would be any good at all. You are the
reason I get up each day. You and the kids.
Yours always,
Frank

Tears welled up as I pulled out Mother's Day
cards made with macaroni and glitter, and
Thanksgiving turkeys traced around Mikey's little
palm print and then mine. She seemed to have
saved everything we ever gave her. I grinned at
my own child scrawl in crayons. I showed a
fondness for purple. Mike seemed to prefer doing
his cards in brown and green. He was colorblind.

Next I found a shoebox from a pair of kids'
shoes. I opened it, expecting to find my baby
shoes, but instead discovered dried rose petals. I
covered the shoebox and looked back inside the
bigger carton.

I dug still deeper. Then I frowned. Down at the
very, very bottom was a manila file folder. I pulled
it out and looked in. Inside were several cards—
Hallmarks. I opened one of the red envelopes. It
was a mushy card about "Loving you so much"
and it was signed "Andrew."

I dropped the card in my lap. Who the hell was

Andrew? And whoever he was, could he be my father? I took a big swig of my stolen pinot noir. Sooner or later, I would have to ask my father about the past. And Frank Quinn was not exactly the most forthcoming man in the world. We had a "don't ask, don't tell" policy in the Quinn family.

But now I would have to ask.

And I prayed he would, for once, tell.

The next morning the alarm rang way too early. Between the long round trip to Little Siberia and the mystery of "Andrew" I was exhausted. I'd slept fitfully, and I didn't feel like getting out of bed, but I never call in sick.

Funny, but my father and brother have never worked an honest day in their lives. They don't operate in the nine-to-five world. But I'm up before 5:00 a.m. each day. Or pretty close to it. I've operated in a very exacting universe. To a criminalist, every analysis has to be painstakingly accurate. Every sample must be treated with sanctity.

I got out of bed, showered and dressed for work. Then I fed my cat and headed to the lab, making it there by quarter after seven. I used my key pass to get in the building, and of course at

the log-in sheet I could see that I hadn't beaten
Lewis there at all. Never have.

I grabbed a cup of coffee from the small
kitchen on our floor—he always starts a pot when
he gets in, and there are usually doughnuts or ba-
gels—and went to his office to say hello.

"Hello, Wilhelmina."

I rolled my eyes. "Hello, Lewis."

"How was the rest of your weekend?"

I slumped into one of the chairs opposite him
and took him step by step through my weekend,
right through to the cards I found.

"Why now? Why has the killer picked now to
try to taunt me?"

Lewis shook his head. "And the lock of hair?
The blood samples?"

"I put them in for processing. Don't know
anything yet."

"How are we doing on the rape kits?"

I shrugged. "It's like shoveling shit against the
tide."

"Well, aren't you going to ask me how my
weekend was?"

"Do I want to know?"

"Mitch and the vice president of the network

took me to dinner at one of the restaurants in the Time Warner building. Japanese place."

I shrugged. "We had Japanese on Friday."

"Yeah. But not bluefin tuna. Exotic sushi. Bill was six hundred dollars each. Each. Not that they let me pay. You need to put four hundred dollars on a credit card just to reserve your table."

"Since when were you impressed by money? You don't spend the money you have now!"

"I know, but it's nice to be wined and dined like a big-shot once in a while instead of fielding calls from crabby prosecutors and assorted politicos who want to bitch at me."

"Lewis, please don't abandon me." As soon as the words left my mouth, I regretted them. "I'm sorry. That's not fair."

"What if you came with me? What if I told them I'd only do it if you were part of my team? Can't you just see us having our own television show? And honey, you'd be a helluva lot better than that Nancy Grace. My God, but it's all I can do but reach through the television and squeeze her neck."

I shook my head. "Lewis, I'm a lab rat. Always have been." I sipped my coffee, then stood up. "I better go." I left Lewis's office and wandered over to my own. Lewis was a lab rat, too. Albeit a more flamboyant one. I just hoped he realized that. I looked around the lab. I couldn't imagine this place without him.

Chapter 8

Kenora Simmons lived in a much nicer place
than I did.

I sat outside her house and tried to fathom how
a twenty-year-old girl from the projects with, as
the cops might say, "no visible means of support," owned an attractive Tudor with four bedrooms and an expansive yard in Englewood
Cliffs. I'd looked it up on the Internet. The house
was worth nearly seven hundred thousand dollars.

The trees on her property were in full bloom, and

pink roses grew up a trellis leading to the second floor. I had been watching her house since I left work at six that Monday. I was just about to call it an evening and go grab some takeout. One of the members of the camera crew was with me to get some footage of the "leg work" involved with cold cases and the Justice Foundation. We'd been driving each other crazy with hunger, trying to decide what kind of food we wanted for dinner. We had settled on Thai and my mouth was watering.

I had tracked down Kenora through one of her old pals from the projects. Just as I checked my watch yet again, Kenora drove up to her house in a flashy red Mustang. Something wasn't right here.

"Nice wheels," the cameraman said. His name was Charlie.

"Nice wheels indeed."

She exited her car, and I climbed out of mine. "Kenora!"

She turned her head toward me. I was stunned. The Kenora of the trial was a plain, African-American girl with hair braided at home by her aunt and a cheap wardrobe. She had been a bit overweight, and the word that came to mind when I saw photos of her was *sloppy*. The prosecutors had encouraged her to dress demurely, I'm sure. And she had tried. But, simply put, taken as a whole, she'd appeared slovenly, as if she hadn't been able to quite figure out how to pull all the elements together.

The woman in front of me now was stunning. If she hadn't had Kenora's hazel eyes, I would have assumed I had the wrong person. She had lost forty pounds, I guessed. Her outfit was impeccable, clearly designer all the way, right down to her "it" bag of the moment, a Chanel. Her hair had been chemically straightened and lightened to a champagne blond, and the effect was gorgeous. Her hair looked silky and swayed across her back as she walked.

She glared at me. "Who are you?"

I crossed the street and walked closer to her. "My name's Billie Quinn." When I was a few feet away from her, it was clear her clothes were absolutely top designer—not knock-off. I was pretty sure she was wearing a Versace pantsuit. But it was the cut, the fit, that told me it was a real name label. It draped her like second skin.

"And?" She stuck her hand on her hip. "You from a record label?"

"No. I'm from the Justice Foundation. We absolutely want to respect what you've been through, Kenora."

She eyed me suspiciously. "Huh?"

"We've reopened the Marcus Hopkins case in an effort to clear his name."

She blinked hard a couple of times, then turned on her Manolo heels and started toward her house.

"Please, Kenora. I just need ten minutes to review your story."

She wheeled around and charged toward me. "I said everything I'm going to say. Everything I was supposed to say. Now you get the fuck away from me, bitch."

"Supposed to say?" I asked her incredulously. "What does that mean?"

She took three strides to me and raised a hand. She was about to claw me with two-inch acrylic nails.

"Whoa, what are you hiding?" I snapped, then I ducked. She then grabbed me by my hair. Out of the corner of my eye, I saw Charlie running his camera.

Kenora yanked my hair for all it was worth, and I screamed and felt tears burning my eyes.

With my left hand, I shot my fist into her stomach, hoping to get her to release my hair. She did, as she doubled over, and I stood up and backed away, but she wasn't done yet. She hurled a few curses at me and then swung her bag, which landed against my face. And I guessed by the pain she'd managed to hit me right where her cell phone was.

Charlie pulled out a cell phone of his own. "I'm gonna call the cops."

Somehow I always cringe at the thought of the cops. I backed away. "Just a minute, Charlie. Look, Kenora, we're just going to leave. Let's just calm down."

Suddenly, though, a burly bodyguard-type in a suit came bursting out of the house. I ducked to avoid Kenora's flailing hands as she came at me again. I backed up out of her range as the guy in the suit came charging at me, barking at Kenora to go inside the house.

"You're on private property. Get off before I call the cops," the burly guy said, a veritable Sherman tank of muscles.

"I just wanted to ask her a question. And I'm in the street. It's public property."

"You can contact her lawyer if you got questions."

"Who's that?"

"Tony Gergen."

I blinked. Gergen was an awfully high-priced lawyer for a girl from the projects who'd somehow hit it big.

Kenora was now standing behind this big guy, who, I could tell from the bulge under his suit jacket, was packing a weapon.

"Tell that bitch to go home, T.C."

"Go in the house, Kenora," he ordered.

I figured I had one last chance to make an appeal to her conscience. "If Marcus didn't do it, Kenora, you ruined one man's life for things, for money. It's not worth your soul."

I saw her face react—her eyes closed slowly and she inhaled and then tightened her lips—but she turned away. T.C. watched as she huffed and then reluctantly went inside like a two-year-old with a tantrum. Then he came close to me. "I see you again, it's trouble."

He patted his side, where he was wearing his gun.

"If she lied, I don't care who you are or what kind of gun you're wearing, big guy," I said icily.

I turned around and stormed toward my car. Charlie had caught everything on videotape— and at that moment, the big guy realized it.

"I want that film."

"Yeah, right," I snorted, turning around again.

He jogged over to Charlie and me. "I said give me the fucking film." He jabbed his index finger right below my collarbone.

"No!" I snapped back and tried to raise myself an inch or two in height. "So back off."

He shoved me, hard, against the car, then grabbed the lens of Charlie's camera and pulled.

Charlie, with the camera mounted on his shoulder, was off balance and he tumbled to the road. I kicked the big guy in the shins. He returned that move with another shove, and I fell back against the hood of my car and wrenched my back.

I watched as he kicked the camera and then opened up the side and yanked out the film. I jumped on his back.

"That belongs to us!" I tried to reach around and grab the film, but he threw me off like I was a tiny spider riding on his back. I fell to the ground.

By this time, Charlie had gotten up. I scrambled to my feet, but the guy was already crossing the street and not looking back.

"Should we call the police?" Charlie asked.

"Nah," I shook my head. "By the time they get here the film will be destroyed already. Besides, we got what we needed."

"We didn't get anything," Charlie said, looking down at his camera and making sure it still worked.

"Yeah, we did. We know she lied. For money. Now we just have to figure out for whom."

"Jesus!" Charlie said, his voice a little hoarse. "This camera's worth a fortune." He pressed some buttons. "It still works, thank God."

Charlie and I got back in our car. I was moving kind of stiffly, and my back hurt like hell. "You still want Thai?" I asked him.

"Yeah, I'm still starving. Upset, but starving. Pissed, but starving."

I drove toward Ft. Lee. "I'm buying. Sorry about that whole thing. I wish it had gone better."

"Are you kidding? Too bad he got the tape. It was awesome footage. Kind of like *Cops.*"

"Great," I said unenthusiastically.

"No, you don't understand, Billie. Every time

we run a Justice Foundation piece, we get tons of
e-mails and stuff at the show. You and Lewis and
Joe are getting pretty damn famous. You're getting
a lot of attention. And some of the e-mails…you've
got some male admirers."

A bolt of realization went through me.

I had an epiphany.

That was why I got the letter from my mother's
killer. He wanted fame. And when he saw me on
television, he realized that what had eluded him
all these years was within his grasp. The Suicide
King case, the Marcus Hopkins case, were
making the Foundation team household names.
And now the killer wanted to be one, too.

Chapter 9

On Wednesday it was another scorcher. All of New York and New Jersey were waiting for a big rain storm to blow through and cool things off, but none was in sight. Each day I'd watch the weatherman as he predicted more cloudless skies, all the while smiling cheerfully when most of us were feeling rather homicidal from the heat.

The lab, in contrast, was icy cold—and for that I was thankful. We always joked that it was like a meat locker...or cold enough for a morgue.

Gallows humor. Over time most criminalists adopted something of a morbid sense of the absurd. I got in to the lab around seven that morning, and of course Lewis was there already, looking smug.

"What?" I snapped at him. "Discover the cure for cancer? The secret of life? The key to immortality?"

"None of the above, but I do have a secret. But what's eating you, besides the obvious?"

"Oh, I don't know…I just love sitting around waiting for a serial killer to decide to contact me again, hoping against all hope he screws up so I can nail him. Meanwhile, you're being wined and dined on thousand-dollar sushi."

"Speaking of which, you and I are going out to dine on raw fish tonight."

"Sushi."

"As a matter of fact, yes."

"I can't afford your new tastes. What was it? A cool five hundred for the privilege of walking into that place?"

"My dime. And not that place. We're going to our usual in Ft. Lee."

"Are you going to tell me why?"

"No."

"But my guess is it has something to do with you looking like the cat that ate the canary."

"Since when do I need a reason to go out to eat with you?"

"Since you became 'Hollywood LeBarge.' I'm not going to jump ship to a television show, Lewis."

"I know, Wilhelmina. Just shut up and come to dinner."

The day passed by in a blur. As many people as I could spare were processing rape kits, and the sheer number of the backlog was both staggering and depressing. One of my cousins was raped when she was nineteen. She went on a date with a guy she met at college. Had two drinks over dinner, decent conversation, but he wasn't her type, she'd decided. A little too cocky and entitled. Later he acted like he was driving her home but instead took her to an isolated lover's lane and raped her.

She told me, then her brother and father. With the last name Quinn, she didn't bother going to police: her dad—my uncle Eddie—took one look at her bruised lip and bite mark on her neck, and he went to the college, tracked down her rapist and beat him, breaking both the guy's legs with a bat and bursting his spleen.

My cousin Tara was never the same after it. She was jumpy, didn't trust anyone. Dropped out of school. She still has to know someone really, really well before she'll even consider a date. When I look at the backlog of rape kits, all the creeps going free while politicians argue over budgets for DNA testing, I can't say I'm sorry my uncle chose to handle it the way he did. Eddie didn't get caught, either. Told the creep that if he said who'd done it, next time four of her cousins would come for him and slice his testicles off. So the guy played it off like a random mugging.

By six that night I was thoroughly tired and emotionally drained. Lewis came to collect me, and I followed his car to Ft. Lee and our usual spot. I still had no idea what Lewis was up to.

The two of us walked into the restaurant, and Lewis waved at a man sitting at a table near the back. I followed Lewis, and the man stood, placed his palms together and bowed to Lewis, who did the same in return.

"Billie, may I present Ben Sato. Detective Ben Sato."

I was going to put my hand out, but I gave a

little bow instead when I saw that was what he was going to do.

"Please, sit down," Detective Sato said. He was an Asian man, unusually tall—maybe six feet two inches. He was dressed in a navy-blue suit that was well tailored to his trim physique, with the crispest, whitest shirt I had ever seen and an intricate geometric-pattern tie in blues and greens. He had black hair cropped very close to his scalp, making him appear almost bald in a cool rock-star kind of bald way—and high cheekbones, with a devilish smile that kind of made his eyes dance. His eyes were black and when he looked at me, I felt as if he was seeing me in my underwear. I don't mean in a lascivious way, but in a way in which his gaze seemed like a human lie detector, intense and honest.

I sat and looked at Lewis, waiting, in my usual way when dealing with the eccentric Mr. LeBarge, for an explanation. Sure enough, he started talking in his usual fashion, sounding ever so slightly like the hybrid child of a used-car salesman and a Southern lawyer.

"Wilhelmina, darlin', Ben and I go way back. Was a time when Tommy Two Trees needed a favor in New Jersey, and Ben here was the police detective who helped him."

Tommy Two Trees was an FBI agent who helped us solve the Suicide King case. He was a big bear of a man—part African-American, part Native American, one hundred percent the real deal.

"Ben, Tommy and I all went out for a proverbial bender. We discussed life, God, Buddha, women and Occam's Razor, among other things. And we've been comrades ever since. You need a detective, so I got you one, Billie. Voilà. Your detective. Now you get to be somebody else's headache for a while."

"I don't need a detective," I snapped at him.

"I told you she was a bit ornery." Lewis smiled at Ben, speaking in an affected whisper as if I was some delusional woman.

The detective stifled a grin. But there his eyes danced again.

"Look, Mr. Sato," I said, "I'm not sure what false pretense Lewis brought you here on, but I'm sure my cold case isn't your top priority."

The waiter came over, and Ben ordered, apparently in fluent Japanese. Lewis ordered me a sake and him a Kirin.

"The sake will help her mellow out," Lewis

said. "I find it's really essential. The Kirin's to help me deal with her."

I punched him on his thigh underneath the table. "Ouch!" Lewis said, quite loudly. Ben Sato had a bemused expression.

After our waiter went back to the bar area, Ben looked poised to say something but he kept silent for a time, and I glanced at Lewis and noticed that he wasn't rushing to shoot off at the mouth the way he usually did. He was being, dare I say, for Lewis, patient. So I waited.

Finally the guy started talking. "I came here eight years ago from Japan. There, very little crime exists. You can walk the streets of even the biggest cities in an atmosphere of peace. No fear."

I thought about the streets of some of the neighborhoods where my father and brother operated. Peace and safety weren't what came to mind.

"I realized," Ben said softly, "that I was living in a state of perpetual irony. I was called to be a warrior in a place that didn't need one. And so eventually I came here."

"And met Lewis, of all people," I said dryly.

"And met Lewis," he replied. He smiled at me. "I think of Lewis as a warrior, too."

"Yeah, he's a warrior all right. Has he shown you his brain collection yet?"

Ben nodded. "Lewis is admittedly a different sort of warrior. Now tell me…from the beginning."

I looked across the table at him. I had nothing to lose, and Lewis was right. I needed someone inside the police department to help me resurrect the trail.

Ben Sato wasn't like any other detective I had ever been around, who usually punctuated and interrupted people's sentences or asked lots of questions. Ben sat back and just listened in complete silence. He didn't interrupt, he didn't stop me to ask me to fill in any blanks. He didn't take notes. And so in one fell swoop, I told him about my mother's disappearance, about my father's "career" and how that meant the police weren't all that interested in the case, on through the long dormancy until the Suicide King case and my appearances on television, to now receiving the letter, being left the souvenir, the incident at the warehouse and, finally, the possibility that my mother had an affair with a mysterious man named Andrew.

When I was finished, he didn't say anything, which was disconcerting. I didn't know whether that meant he thought I was out of my mind, or whether he thought the killer really was returning to torment me.

I looked over at Lewis, who seemed completely unperturbed that Ben was so silent. I tried not to look irritated.

Our waiter approached our table and took our sushi orders. Ben again ordered in Japanese. Lewis ordered a spider roll.

"Don't tell Ripper," he told me.

Ignoring him, I ordered a tuna sashimi dinner. And then, finally, Ben looked me in the eyes.

"There is nothing worse than a family left without resolution. I believe it's like the Greek myth of Achlys. Do you know it?"

I shook my head.

"She was the first being ever in existence, born into perpetual darkness and despair, doomed to perpetual sorrow and crying. When she's represented in Greek art, to me, she is grief personified. You are like Achlys. Perpetual darkness and sorrow until we find the killer and you can move beyond the dark realm."

I glanced over at Lewis, my brows knit together. Another one of Lewis's mythology-spouting pals. He seemed to gravitate toward them. But, like Tommy Two Trees, I sensed Ben was a man of his word, a warrior. So now I had a new partner to sift through the dust of the past to try to solve my mother's murder.

"That sums up how I feel sometimes. Wandering in perpetual grief."

"We start tomorrow," Ben said resolutely.

I nodded and promised Ben I would meet him the next night at nine at a bar in Hoboken after I visited my father. I was supposed to bring Ben all my research, summarized, which was easy to do. For as long as I had been trying to piece together my mother's murder, I had kept neat file cabinets filled with press clippings, theories, notes and interviews. As I became more computer savvy, I had scanned most of it and compiled it by subject.

I looked over at Lewis. He had found me a warrior, not unlike myself, Lewis, C.C., Joe.

And a warrior was what I needed. Perhaps now I would get the answers that had eluded me my whole life.

Chapter 10

My father has never been what you might term forthcoming about his life. I understand why, of course. But I knew if I was going to bury my mother—really bury her in peace—then he and I were going to have to lay all our cards on the table once and for all.

I pulled into my father's driveway early the next evening, parked and got out. The air was stifling, and I wished the approaching sundown was going to cool things, but I knew it wasn't. I took a deep breath and strode up the slate walkway and into my childhood home, musing for probably the thousandth time how little had changed about it.

We lived in a typical suburb of manicured lawns and white picket fences when I was young. My father chose our town for its good schools and chose our house so Mom and he could fill it with children and she could have a garden. It was a big Dutch Colonial with five bedrooms and hardwood floors and real plaster walls. A picture window looked out the front, and there was a treehouse hidden in the old oak tree in the backyard that extended to "the woods." When I was little, it seemed like an impenetrable forest, but it was actually just a hundred-year flood line, so no houses were allowed to be built back there.

When I entered the house, I looked at the wooden staircase leading upstairs, pegs on the wall opposite it. Now my father's jacket hung from one peg and his keys from another, but when Mikey and I were little, the foyer was a messy zone of childhood. Our coats, galoshes, lunchboxes and book bags were always scattered, along with baseball gloves for my brother and library books for me.

"Dad?" I called out.

"In here," he called back.

I wandered into the kitchen. He was standing over a pot of boiling water. Spaghetti with jar sauce was about the extent of his cooking repertoire—and mine, come to think of it.

"Hey, Daddy." I smiled at him and walked over to kiss his cheek. The kitchen was right out of the seventies. He had never bothered to update it. The countertops were avocado green, and though he'd gotten new appliances over the years as things broke down, he still had the old-fashioned range from when my mom was alive. The effect was kind of kitschy.

"Hi. Garlic bread is in the oven, if I don't burn it. Sit down. Wine is breathing. Your brother will be here in about ten minutes."

I sat at the long rectangular table and poured myself a glass of red wine—not so coincidentally the same vintage as my likely stolen Australian brand.

"Dad...I went up to Little Siberia on Sunday."

"God, what a hellhole."

"Yeah, pretty much.... You know Marty O'Hare's doing his time there, right?"

"Yeah. Poor son of a bitch. I hate the bastard, but…even he deserves better than Dannemora."

"He got a message to me. I think he just wants to get under your skin. Something about Mom having an affair." I decided to leave out the doubts about my parentage for now.

Dad had been stirring the pot of pasta, but he stopped. "That prick. Bothering you with that bullshit."

"So there's something to it?" I asked. I held my wineglass by the stem and twirled it, barely breathing while I waited for his answer.

"No. There's nothing to it. Before your mother met me, she dated this guy for a long time. He had a scholarship to Yale, real smart guy. Old money. That's who her parents wanted her to marry."

"Really?" This was the first I'd heard of it. After my mother's death, my maternal grandparents passed away within two years—I think the strain of losing her was a big factor. "Were you jealous of him?"

Dad turned to face me, anger visible on his face. "Yes."

My insides crumbled. Could my father have killed her? Even accidentally, in a rage?

"You were?" I managed to say, though my throat was dry despite the wine.

"Yes. Who wouldn't be? Your mother was beautiful. She was the most perfect woman ever. And I'm not just saying that because she passed away, Billie. She was. Did you know I used to bring her a red rose every single Friday?"

That explained the shoebox of roses.

He sighed, releasing the tension in his jaw. "Of course I was jealous. And this guy and your mother had a history. My own in-laws thought I was no good. And he could have given her a more…normal life. I mean, that's half the reason I bought this big old house for her. I never wanted her to feel like she lost out by marrying a crook like me."

"She never felt that way, Dad. I'm sure she didn't."

"I know. But people talked. You know how the guys can be."

"Yeah." I knew amongst my father and brother and their crew how the ribbing was both sophomoric and intense at times.

"But it was bullshit. And that's why I just… well, I knew even though Daniel ran into her a few

times when she would go to Ridgewood to visit
her parents, that I had nothing to worry about. She
and I were destiny."

"Daniel?"

"Yeah. Daniel Carter. He owns that huge
shopping plaza over in Ridgewood. A bunch of
other property, too. Kind of a real estate tycoon."

I blinked hard a few times. Who the hell was
Andrew, then? How many secrets was my
mother hiding?

"Does the name Andrew mean anything to you,
Dad?"

He shook his head. "Nope. Why?"

"Oh…nothing. I thought that was what Marty
O'Hare said, but I guess I was wrong."

"Good thing that asshole is in Little Siberia or
I'd kill him with my bare hands…. Oh, good…
your brother is here."

I stifled a smile. That was Dad.

Mikey came in, kissed the top of my head,
grabbed a cold beer from the fridge and sat down
at the table.

"So what's up, Billie? And where's David?"

I shrugged. "He's been so involved with this
law school stuff. I don't know. And it hasn't been

easy adjusting to being around each other. He's still very closed in a lot of ways. Always on guard. Can't sleep."

Dad brought over the garlic bread—fairly burnt but still smelling delicious. "Well, you just be patient, Billie. He's a good man."

Next he came over to the table with the pasta and Ragu sauce. He sometimes tosses in some oregano and ground beef to try to doctor it a little. It doesn't taste half bad.

"I have to tell you both something," I said quietly once we all started eating.

"What?" My father's voice had a hint of anxiety to it. He's never been totally comfortable with the Justice Foundation.

"Well...I got a letter from someone who claimed to know what happened to Mom."

My father's face flushed. "Some crackpot?"

"No," I said gently. "Inside the letter was a scrap of her dress fabric. And then a few days later, I was followed to the shooting range and left a souvenir. I'm not sure who it belonged to—but it was human hair."

Mikey put down his fork and looked queasy.

"I'm sorry," I said. "I shouldn't have done this

over dinner. I just wanted you two to know that the attention the Justice Foundation has maybe gotten has caught the eye of whoever killed her or a witness. And I'm going to figure out who he is. I even have a homicide detective willing to help."

"Well, I know you don't want to hear this, but I think Tommy Salami should take you to and from work for a while," Dad said.

"You know," I told him, "I'm not sure that's such a good idea. Let's discuss that some other time, okay? For now, is there anything either of you can think of, anything at all that you think I should know about that night?"

Dad shook his head. "I wasn't even around. I was on the docks meeting with some longshore-men about gambling receipts from their union when it happened."

Mikey sipped his beer. "I don't like to think about it."

"I know. I don't either," I said.

"That's not true, Billie. Your entire career is about DNA and crimes. Everything about you has to do with her. It's who you are—you think about it all the time."

It sounded almost like an accusation. "Mikey...

I thought you would want to catch whoever it is. Why don't you understand that?"

"I do. I just hate thinking about it, that's all. I barely remember that night. You say you remember a man in the house. I don't. I remember going up to bed and her coming and tucking me in. And then next thing I remember is the cops giving me milk and feeding me cookies. Then the funeral and everything."

"You don't remember her talking to someone in the house?"

He shook his head. "The only weird thing I remember is she had on her pearls. I remember because I was playing with them when she bent over to kiss me good night. But she wasn't dressed for pearls. Like why put on your best jewelry if you're just vacuuming and stuff?"

He had never mentioned this detail before. And I had no obvious answer. Had she donned the pearls for Daniel? For my father? For Andrew?

I looked from my father to my brother and back again, and I felt very alone. I couldn't tell them that as much as I wanted to solve my mother's murder, I also wanted to find out if I was even a Quinn after all.

Chapter 11

Ben Sato took the CD-ROM I handed him. He smiled his enigmatic smile, gave a little bow and gestured to the booth he had reserved for us.

"Nice place," I murmured. "I've never been in here before."

"I like it because it's quiet. And they play jazz."

"You like jazz?"

He nodded, sitting down. "I like Charlie Parker. And Billie Holiday."

"A little melancholy," I mused.

"So am I," he said.

There was a moment of silence between us. I realized that I was going to have to get used to silences if I was going to work with him.

"I brought my laptop," he said, pulling out a Sony Vaio from the bench next to him and putting it on the table. He took the CD from its jewel case and after firing up the PC, popped it in.

"You're thorough." He said it as a compliment.

On the CD I had dozens and dozens of files, labeled clearly, such as, "Interview notes neighbor," or "newspaper clippings." I had scanned all of our newspapers from that time and made PDF files. I had interviewed and reinterviewed all the neighbors from that time. I had files with digital pictures of the house, as well as files with digital pictures of the woods where she was found.

"I should have guessed. Criminalists are exacting."

I nodded.

"You could have been a homicide detective."

"Not if I wanted to remain in the family. My father and brother wouldn't be too pleased. I mean, it's bad enough I work in a crime lab. It would be another thing entirely to be a cop. The

Quinns are from the other side of the law. My uncle Sean's serving life for murder. But you know all that already."

He smiled. "How do you know?"

"Because I can tell you didn't come into that meeting with me and Lewis blind. You looked into me. My family. The case. That would be how you handled it. Am I right? Thorough. Exacting."

I was going to say anal retentive, but decided not to. In Ben's case, I thought his nature was about respecting the victim of the crime, being sure he left no stone unturned.

He nodded.

"I still don't get why you came to the United States. Boredom? Ennui?"

"A warrior with no war."

"And why take my cold case?"

He didn't say anything. He opened file after file, studying, memorizing—I could just see that about him. He was committing everything to memory. I was sure of it.

A waitress came over, and I ordered a bourbon and soda. He ordered a single-malt scotch. I waited patiently while he went through each and every file.

"My sister was killed." He said it quietly, and

it took me a minute to realize he was referring to himself, revealing something personal.

"I'm sorry."

"Crime is so rare. When it happens, it's an affront to our whole society. But justice in Japan is different. It took me six years to catch her murderer. And then I came here. I suppose I was frustrated by justice there. The process."

"I'm sorry."

"She was murdered by a very rich man's son. A billionaire. His position meant special treatment. No arrest for a very long time even though it was quite clear he killed her for fun."

"Rich people and celebrities get special treatment here, too."

"I know. But in the ideal, justice wears a blindfold."

"I wish it always worked that way."

"We must try to be impartial, to strive for the ideal." He looked me in the eyes. "So I understand what it's like to want to solve a case like this. Something personal."

"To leave the place of perpetual despair," I said, remembering his mythology.

"Exactly."

Our drinks arrived, and I sipped mine. "I feel like one day I'm going to look at those files and see something that's been there all along. Like searching for something you've lost and it's been right under your nose the whole time."

"Tell me about the letter you got at work."

"Well, there's more now." I took Ben through receiving the letter, the attack at the shooting range, and the letters from Andrew kept separately, as well as my mother's first love, Daniel. I even told him about my father and the message from Marty O'Hare.

"You must do two things. You must test your DNA against your father's. And you must find Daniel."

"You think it's a personal crime?" I asked him.

"Statistically you know that to be so. But evil doesn't pay attention to statistics. So, we have to check it as a process of elimination."

I looked at him. His face was unreadable in many ways. "After you found her killer, were you able to find peace?"

He shut his eyes for a moment. "Peace…is something within. I am the ultimate paradox. At peace when I am at war."

"At war against evil."

He nodded. "I feel like a perpetual soldier."

A paradox. That was what my life was. I freed a man, but we were both imprisoned by our pasts. I was a criminalist, a scientist, who had decided to make DNA personal. And it was only a matter of time before I found out just how personal it was.

Chapter 12

Kenora called my cell phone on Friday—she had called the Foundation's office and gotten my number. The two of us agreed to meet at an out-of-the-way bar up in Suffern, New York. Suffern was an exit off of the New York State Thruway—a town accessible to the highway. She suggested the place. It wasn't likely she or I would run into anyone we knew.

The bar was in a strip mall, and Irish shamrocks were painted on the windows. I walked in at eight that night. I had come alone, as she asked me to. She was waiting in a back booth.

I fitted in at the bar she chose. Not because I was white or most of the bar's patrons were white, or even because I was Irish, but because I had on jeans and a tank top with a black linen jacket, my hair in a ponytail, no makeup on, sneakers on my feet. I knew I was attractive—but my kind of beauty is simple—long shiny hair, good complexion, nice smile, good body. Kenora, the "new and improved" Kenora, didn't fit in because she was so extraordinary. She looked like she had just stepped off a tour bus as a music star. When I reached the table, I saw that tonight she had in color contacts that transformed her eyes to an exotic emerald color, and her body-hugging outfit seemed to have been sewn precisely to fit her. I sat down without waiting to be asked.

"Hi," I said. I had checked out the place from the parking lot. I hadn't seen any bodyguard types.

"Thanks for coming," she said softly.

"I'm still not sure why you wanted to meet me."

She looked down at the table but didn't say anything.

I waited, but still nothing. Finally, I spoke.

"Kenora," I exhaled, trying to gather my thoughts. "I didn't grow up in the projects. So I don't know what it's like to have the deck stacked against me in terms of race and poverty and education. I don't want to screw up the life you have, no matter how you got it. I believe you were raped."

"I was."

I nodded. "But Marcus's blood wasn't on you. And the stain isn't your blood, either. And he *had* an alibi. So here's the thing, Kenora. I may not have grown up in the projects, but my mother was murdered. The case was never solved. And that deck was stacked against me my whole life. I never got over it. I'm still not over it."

She swallowed hard. "How was she killed?"

"Not sure. She disappeared and they didn't find her for months."

"Did your daddy do it? That happened to a friend of mine. Her boyfriend, Derek, didn't want to get married when he got her pregnant, so Derek killed her. And there was a girl in the building next to mine whose husband killed her 'cause he found out his baby wasn't really his."

For the first time in my entire life, I didn't

know how to answer the question of my father's guilt or innocence. "I don't think my dad had anything to do with it."

Kenora looked down at the glass of champagne she had in front of her. The waitress came over and I ordered a cola. After the waitress left, neither I nor Kenora said anything for a few minutes. Finally I decided to take the lead.

"Marcus didn't do it, did he?"

She was very still, but after a long pause, she shook her head.

"Do you want to tell me who did?"

"I'm not a bad person."

I nodded at her. "You're here now. Kenora, you can fix this."

Her hands shook, and she took a big swig of her drink. "I was raped by Tony Castle."

I had to conceal my reaction. Tony Castle was a major NBA player, drafted after his sophomore year in college. He had endorsement deals for sneakers, a car, a soft drink, a sports drink. He was a huge star in the sports world. "Was he from your neighborhood?" I tried to remember his story beyond the ghetto-to-NBA, rags-to-riches inspirational stuff that they always talked about on sports shows or during games.

"Way back. I mean, way, way back. See—" she took another swig of champagne "—he was from the same projects. But he left. Went to live with his coach. That was his shot, you know?"

I nodded, urging her with my eyes to go on.

"He used to come back once in a while, not often, to play b-ball with his old friends. One time he did, he kept flirting with me. Next thing I knew, he went nuts. Said I was a tease and a whore and a gold digger. He raped me." She wiped at a stray tear. "His friend Curtis watched. Didn't do anything except occasionally say, 'Go for it, Tony.'"

I was afraid to breathe, afraid any word from me might stop her from telling her story.

"I was hurt. He punched me in the stomach. Hurt real bad. I went home, cleaned up 'cause I felt so disgusting. I didn't tell anyone. He told me not to. Then I changed my mind. Like…at first I wasn't going to say anything, but then I felt really angry and I went to the police. Then his agent comes to me. Comes to my aunt's house—I lived with her. Says he has a deal for me. If I say Marcus did it, then I'll get paid. Not a little bit of money, either. 'Cause it turns out the draft was coming up. And they didn't want this story breaking and maybe messing things up."

"But why Marcus?"

"I think they picked him because he had no record. Figured he'd beat it. I don't know. I didn't ask. I just did like I was told. My aunt told me this was my chance to get out."

"But when you filed the report, didn't you give a description? Marcus is nowhere near as tall as Tony Castle. Didn't you give a name?"

She nodded. "I did, but that file somehow got lost or something. I think they bought the police off, too. I mean, I didn't think it at first. I just thought it was just them thinking some bitch from the projects got raped, so who cares. But now I'm not so sure. That first report was never filed. The cops went after Marcus."

"So why now? Why come forward after all this time?"

"'Cause they gave me a lot of money. And my aunt. And even Curtis. And I took my money and moved away. I got pretty." She ran her fingers through her hair. "But no matter what I did, I still felt ugly inside. And it got to me. The guilt. So I want to fix this. Hopefully without going to prison. Or getting myself killed."

"How much money were you paid?"

"Four million dollars."

"Jesus!"

She nodded. "His contract was worth $76 million. And I heard he paid off one other woman, too. And that's not counting all the money he gets saying those sneakers are going to make some kid jump higher if he pays two hundred dollars for 'em. And he does a bunch of commercials. He's loaded."

"I know." I tried to imagine the legal team this guy would have. "Are you willing to meet with Joe Franklin? Do you know who he is?"

"Yeah. Do you think he can keep me out of prison?"

"He'll try to get you the best deal possible. In all of this, you were an impressionable rape victim. This agent pulling the strings, Tony Castle himself, they're the most culpable."

"I just want to breathe again. Without the guilt. Sleep one night without thinkin' of Marcus in prison."

I pulled out my cell phone and called Joe. I gave

him the short version of events. He gave me instructions, and I disconnected and faced her again.

"He says to go to his office tomorrow. Here's his card." I fished a business card out and handed it to her. "But you go to this corporate office, not the Justice Foundation one. Between now and then, he says don't talk to a soul. Don't tip your hand, nothing. Do you understand, Kenora? When this comes out, there's going to be a firestorm of media like you've never seen before. Joe will help you handle it all, make sure your interests are represented. And the good news is we should be able to get Marcus out really soon."

She looked relieved. "Nothing in my life has been good, really good, since then. I haven't been to church in two years."

"Well, confession is good for the soul, Kenora."

The two of us sat and talked awhile. Lives of desperation lead people to do things they regret, that they're ashamed of. I understood why Kenora did what she did. But I thought of Marcus's pain. I hoped he could somehow repair his life and move on; I hoped bitterness wouldn't consume him.

We settled our bill about an hour later, and I walked Kenora to her fancy car and shook her hand

and wished her luck. "Joe is a really good lawyer—the best—and I know he'll try to help you."

"He won't hate me for what I've done?"

I shook my head. "He wants to help Marcus. But he'll want to make sure that you come through this okay, too."

I waved goodbye as she drove off, climbed in my own car and drove to the entrance to the thruway. I was doing about sixty-five miles an hour when my right rear tire blew. I heard this loud sound like a gunshot, and then felt the car pull into the other lane.

"Jesus!" I shouted, my heart pounding. An eighteen-wheeler was bearing down on me, horn blaring. I struggled to maintain control of the wheel. My old Caddie didn't have antilock brakes, and with such a big car, I was fishtailing. Soon I could feel I was driving on the rim.

With the odd thump-thumping sound of a car with a blown tire, as soon as the eighteen-wheeler barreled past me, I looked for a spot to pull over. In my rearview mirror, I saw sparks trailing in back of me from the rim dragging against the cement road.

My arms shaking from the effort, I finally

pulled over to the side of the thruway. Cars whizzed past me. I knew I could call my brother to come get me and he'd be there as fast as he could. But I also knew how to change a tire myself.

I was well off to the side and put on my hazards, but it was still dangerous at night. I retrieved my gun from the glove compartment. I didn't like feeling so vulnerable. I slipped out of my blazer, and slid across the seat, climbed out on the passenger side and went around to my trunk. As I got closer, I saw something underneath my rear bumper.

"Shit!" I assumed I'd hit something. Maybe that was what had caused my flat.

I squinted in the darkness, the only light coming from the headlights of cars passing me. When I got closer, I could see that whatever it was on my bumper, it was duct taped there.

I knelt down and saw it was another envelope, like the one that had been left for me at the shooting range. I pulled it off and looked inside. Another lock of hair.

Only, this lock was the same shade as my own.

There was a note. Much as I wanted to read it, I wanted to get to the lab with no chance of contaminating it.

I pulled my jack and spare tire out of my trunk, and then, my loaded gun by my side, I changed my tire, sweating in the heat of the summer night. As soon as I got my tire changed, I threw the old tire in the trunk and wiped my dirty hands on my jeans. I took the envelope and my gun, and I climbed back in my car and headed toward the lab.

I had a feeling, a sickening feeling in the pit of my stomach, that the envelope on the seat next to me contained my mother's hair.

Another souvenir.

Despite the work I do, I have never been any closer to understanding the mind of a criminal, the mind of a serial killer. Is it possible to be born without a conscience?

Unlike television shows and movies that play up the role of criminalists, it's not my job to understand the psyche of a killer. That's for the detectives, the D.A., the forensic psychologists and the profilers. My role is about analysis. Taking the genetic fingerprints and running my tests.

But of course, Lewis and I have always been aware of our part, of how we use the detritus of our human DNA to catch evil. The psyche, however, has always puzzled me.

I understand crimes of passion. I understand street crime. Drug crime. Gang violence. I understand crimes born of the kind of mind-numbing poverty Marcus and Kenora grew up in. But serial killers are a breed apart.

I thought of BTK writing chillingly of killing a little girl. Or of Danny Rollins staging his victims. Or of Ted Bundy using his very handsome ordinariness to dupe unsuspecting women. I thought of the German cannibal who struck a bargain with a man who volunteered to be killed.

With these souvenirs, I was being plunged into the strange fantasies of a killer. Like Lewis said, it was cat and mouse.

And right now I had the feeling he was dangling me in his paws.

Chapter 13

I ignored all the missed calls on my cell phone. I knew it was probably David, but I desperately wanted to open the envelope in the lab as soon as possible. I flashed my badge at the night security guard.

"Hey, Carl, how's it going?"

"Good, Billie. You're in late."

I shrugged, carrying the envelope. "I have something I need to look at right away."

"Got a pot of coffee over there, if you want some."

"No, thanks." I waved to him and hurried on to the lab. Once inside, I pulled on rubber gloves and readied a bench where I planned to open the envelope. I turned on the light and took a deep breath.

Close up, under magnifying glass, the hair had flecks of blood on it, just like the other souvenir. But this one really was the exact same shade as my own hair—I felt certain it was from my mother, and hair analysis would hopefully confirm that.

Next, I pulled out the note and carefully unfolded it.

Another present for my darling.
Love,
Daddy

I wanted to throw up. I prepared the sample for analysis, stat. I hoped for a careless fingerprint. A bit of saliva on the envelope. Something. As we walk, as we live our lives, we leave our DNA residue all around us. We literally shed the evidence that can solve a crime.

I left the lab and went to my office. I fired up my computer. While I waited, I recalled the world's most infamous serial killers. From the Zodiac Killer to BTK, Son of Sam to Jack the Ripper, there was a long history of serial killers taunting their pursuers. Some said it was because they secretly longed to get caught. BTK got very sloppy when he came out of seeming retirement and started writing to the newspaper again. He was eventually traced because of a computer disk.

I was convinced that my mother's killer was a sociopath. Only someone like Ted Bundy toys with people, writes notes meant to torment.

Technology was in my favor. On the one hand, a very smart serial killer can always be cautious—use a condom, wipe off prints, wear rubber gloves, burn his clothes. On the other hand, just a fragment is enough, especially with the advances we've made in replicating DNA. Whereas before we needed a fairly pure sample of a certain size—albeit tiny—now we can take the most minute sample and duplicate it again and again.

Why the note? I pondered. I don't know if I believed it was a desire to be caught. I went on the Internet and found one article that agreed with me—an FBI behavioralist who claims it's the killers' own egos, causing them to want to manipulate the press, the police, believing they are invincible. They don't want to get caught—they want to play God. My mother's killer wanted to mess with my mind.

"Daddy."

The killer wasn't just taunting me about her death, he was taunting me about the very doubts that now plagued me concerning my father, which meant he was close enough to my family to know enough about my mother and father to torment me about this. To leave me his souvenirs.

Statistically, I've heard the theories about how many serial killers operate in the United States at any given time. I know that a serial killer can be ordinary. Your neighbor. Your coworker. I shuddered. He was close. I was certain of it.

I'd have to unravel all the threads carefully if I was going to catch him…without being caught in the killer's net myself.

I leaned back in my chair and rubbed my eyes. My cell phone rang again.

"Hello?"

"Billie," David's voice was unusually sharp. "Where have you been?"

I was tired and starting to notice my arms ached from changing the tire on my car. "David, I'm sorry, it's been a long night."

"Jesus Christ! Yeah, it has. A phone call, Billie. A simple phone call so I wouldn't worry."

"Look," I snapped at him. "I don't call you and bitch when you've stayed at the law library all day and evening. I figure you're busy."

"Yeah, but no one at the law library is stalking me, Billie."

"Come on. Some of those librarians are downright dangerous."

"Don't joke. Not about this. Are you coming home?"

I sighed. "Yeah."

"Good. We need to talk."

I closed my phone, but inwardly I moaned. If ever there was a warning sign of trouble in a relationship, it was the "we need to talk" speech.

I left the lab, said good-night to Carl and got in my car for the drive home. Once I got to my street, I scouted for a parking spot. I found one directly under a streetlamp—pure luck—and I parallel parked. On a hunch, when I got out, I opened my trunk and took a closer look in the light at the blown tire. Sure enough, there were three huge nails perfectly spaced apart—deliberate. The bastard could have killed me.

I slammed my trunk shut and then walked to my apartment. When I got to the second floor, I opened the door, and David was waiting.

"Hi," I said wearily. "Do we really have to do the whole talking thing right now?"

"Yes. Billie, I didn't know where you were—and neither did Lewis."

"Joe knew."

"Yeah, well, I didn't. What kind of relationship is this? I'm not your babysitter, but the work you do is pretty intense, Billie. Finding the real Suicide King killer almost killed you. I don't want to risk you not coming home some night."

He was wearing sweatpants and a muscle T-shirt, and his arms were crossed. He had five-o'clock shadow, and part of me just wanted to tell him I loved him and climb into bed with him.

"David, I can't abandon the Justice Foundation. I can't. And I'm going to find out what happened to my mother."

"Even if it gets you killed? Why do you have to do this alone? Why can't I help you?"

"I don't know. It just seems like such a lonely thing. Like something I have to do on my own."

"Ben Sato is helping you." His voice was accusing.

"He's a cop, David. I need his help."

"So. Jack was a cop."

The comment hung there in the air between us, angry and ugly. My ex-boyfriend Jack had been a cop. He'd also been a reluctant accomplice to a killer. And he had framed David.

"That's unfair."

"Losing ten years of my life in a prison hellhole is unfair. I know what unfair is, Billie."

"But I didn't do that to you."

"I know. Your lover did."

The comment knocked my breath out of me. "Don't be like this. Ben Sato is trying to help me."

"I'm sure he is." David's eyes were a mixture of jealousy and anger.

"He's an honorable man."

"He just wants to get you in bed."

"Fuck you, David."

I saw his face crumble. We'd never fought. Not

once. I found it incredible, actually. The Quinns are known for impatience and hot-headedness, and I'm no exception. And it certainly would have been understandable if David's readjustment to freedom had included some moments of hostility. But instead we had always been sexually charged and emotionally supportive.

"I didn't mean that, Billie. I was just mad with worry."

I turned on my heel, and he grabbed my arm.

"Don't!" I seethed and shrugged him off. I called to Bo and put on his leash. "I'm going for a walk."

"Let me come with you."

"No!" I snapped.

"Billie, we're both under a lot of strain. Please..."

"Don't follow me. Let me cool off."

"No—"

Ignoring him, I opened the door and dashed out with Bo. I was trembling with fury. I tried to breathe deeply as I walked, reasoning that we were both under so much stress, with so many obstacles to happiness. I hurried down the stairs and out onto the sidewalk. The air was still stifling. I walked Bo and then settled into a half jog. I glanced at my watch. It was almost midnight. In the distance, I could hear some of the bar patrons on the main drag in Hoboken spilling out of the restaurants and pubs.

I thought of making my way to Quinn's. Maybe a beer and talking to my brother was all I needed. He usually played pool there a couple of nights a week. Mikey had the eternal optimism of a con man, always sure his big break was around the next bend, the next truck he hijacked, the next score. He had an infectious smile, and he made me feel loved.

Having made up my mind to go find my brother, I slowed my pace. And then I heard footsteps behind me.

Glancing ahead of me, I realized the side street I was on was deserted. I was at least twelve blocks from Quinn's. I wanted to turn around and see who was behind me, but this strange feeling in my gut told me not to. That I wouldn't like what I saw.

Grateful for Bo, I picked up my pace. Bo panted beside me, his paws making a clicking sound as he trotted beside me. I could hear that the person in back of me picked up his pace, too. I recalled, in an instant, all the things about street crime drilled into my head by both my father and, actually, Jack—a crooked cop, yes, but he had loved me. I moved off of the sidewalk and into the street, crossing to the other side to see if the person following me did the same. He did.

Staying in the street, rather than on the sidewalk, I looked for a lighted building with people around. A bar. A pub. A convenience store. I couldn't see one. I spotted a well-lit apartment building ahead, and I dashed to its lobby.

Trying the door, I realized, too late, it was one whose security system meant I couldn't get beyond the vestibule—and there was no doorman. I buzzed on all the buzzers to apartments. A woman answered one.

"Hello?" It was the voice of an elderly woman.

"Hi…I'm down in the lobby of your building and someone is following me. Can you buzz me in?" I hoped my voice conveyed the fear I felt.

The woman hesitated. "I'm afraid we've had some break-ins. I can't let you in, but I'll call 911."

"Fine. Please call them then. *Please!*"

Bo was frantic, pacing back and forth, picking up on my anxiety. I was shaking, and I clasped my hands together and breathed in and out a few times to try to calm my adrenaline rush.

I stepped a little closer to the door, in an attempt to peek and see what the man tailing me looked like. It was my friendly, neighborhood, masked freak again. He stepped toward the vestibule.

I was trapped.

Chapter 14

I didn't have my gun. And I was in a vestibule barely big enough to throw a roundhouse kick, if I could even remember to do one properly from the Krav Maga classes I took for exercise a few years back.

I pressed all the buzzers again. I hoped that if I annoyed enough people, they'd *all* call the cops. That's what I wanted…cops swarming the place.

Bo was really untrained—he was a puppy. A

big, sloppy puppy, but now he started barking like an attack dog.

"That's it, boy! That's it. He's a bad guy." Bo strained at his leash. His growls and barking echoed off the tiled walls of the vestibule. "That's it, boy!" He had great instincts. He knew we were in danger.

I decided if I was going to be attacked, I wanted to be on the street where I had a fighting chance. The door swung out, so I positioned myself in such a way that it would swing right into the killer—or at least the creep I thought was the killer.

With all my might, I gave the door a shove. The heavy glass door did push against him, forcing him to take a step or two backwards. I rushed out, with Bo ahead of me, and then I let go of Bo's leash. "Get him, Bo!"

The dog lunged at the creep, barking insanely. Bo was a gentle soul who let my cat sleep on his back. His behavior showed me that his animal instincts were picking up on evil. He bared his teeth, snapping. I reached out to try to grab the mask, but the stalker was flailing, and I couldn't get close to him.

In the distance I heard the wail of sirens. The masked weirdo muttered, "Shit!" He kicked his leg out and hit poor Bo square on the snout. Bo responded by yelping in pain, but then he surprised even me by bounding at the guy and taking a bite of his pant leg. Snarling, Bo tugged hard. I saw the killer getting more frantic. The cops would be there any minute. With one momentous effort, the killer pulled away and dashed down the street, then down an alley. Bo gave chase until I called him back.

"Come on, Bo...good job."

Bo trotted back. My heart was still pounding, but the puppy saved my life. I knelt down to check out his nose, making sure he was okay.

"Hey, Bo...what do you have there?"

In his teeth was a piece of cloth. "You tore his pant leg. Good for you, boy!" I whispered. And then I felt my heart skip a beat. "And it has blood on it."

I had his DNA.

I held the cloth in my hand, as police cars came careening down the street. Two cop cars parked, lights flashing and reflecting off of the glass on the buildings nearby.

"Hey, Officers," I said. "He went that way." I pointed down the street. "Made a left at that alley. He attacked me, so be careful."

Two officers left in pursuit, one came over to me, and the fourth went to call for more backup.

"Hello, ma'am, I'm Officer Parks. Want to tell me what happened here?" He stood about six feet tall, and if he weighed 120 pounds, that was a lot. Skinny but wiry, he had a soft voice and gentle gray eyes.

I knew enough from my time with Jack to know I was best off having a friend navigate this with me—a friend inside the force.

"I'm working with Detective Ben Sato. He's from the Ft. Lee Police Department. I was wondering if you could call him. Tell him Billie Quinn was attacked tonight."

"Sure." He made a call from his cell phone, eventually dialing Ft. Lee's department, and spoke to someone on duty. After he disconnected his cell, he said, "Detective Sato is off duty, but they're calling him at home."

"Can you bag this as evidence?" I handed him the cloth with the blood on it.

"This from the suspect?"

I nodded. "My dog got it."

"Good dog." The officer grinned at Bo. "You saved your lady, here."

"He sure did."

"Are you hurt?"

I shook my head.

"All right, let's start from the beginning here."

The beginning. I'd have to go all the way back over two decades to do that.

I looked around at the gathering crowd. I decided starting at the beginning was way too complicated. I instead opted to take a shortcut until Ben showed up.

"I got in an argument with my boyfriend this evening and went out for a walk with Bo to cool off. I wasn't paying attention, and I realized someone was following me. I felt like I was in danger, so I looked for someplace to call the police or to get around people, and I ended up in that apartment vestibule. Building 609 there. And I buzzed people's apartments until someone answered. I begged her to call 911. And then the guy following me tried to come after me in the vestibule, so I released my dog, who was barking like crazy, and the dog chased him before anything really horrible could happen to me."

"You were lucky."

I nodded.

"You have a description of the guy?"

"He was wearing a mask."

"What kind of mask?"

"A creepy one. Flesh-colored, and it sticks to him."

"How tall?"

"About five-eleven."

"Hair color?"

"Wig."

"You have any idea who might be following you?"

"Technically, no."

"What do you mean?"

Who was I kidding? There was no shortcut. And as soon as I laid this out for this cop, it would eventually make the newspapers. So I lied.

"I mean, no."

He looked like he was about to ask me another question, when the other two officers emerged from the alleyway.

"We saw him. He ditched the wig and got in a car. Too far away to get plates."

The officer, a woman, held up the wig. "We could tell it was a Ford. A blue one. Nondescript. A sedan of some sort. Ask me, it was likely a rental.

Newark airport isn't but ten miles from here. We could make some inquiries. Not much to go on."

Another siren screeched through the night. Backup, and with it, or close behind it, an ambulance.

"Really," I said, "I'm not hurt."

Cars were being stopped and redirected, so traffic no longer was coming down the street—not that there was much at this hour of the morning. A minute or so later, a two-door black Acura pulled up alongside the police cars, and Ben Sato climbed out.

"Ben," I said his name as a rush of relief passed through me. He was dressed in black pants and a black T-shirt, and he confidently strode over, nodded to the officers and pulled me aside. I gave him the story, and he nodded, not speaking. He stared at me, then whispered, "I'm very grateful you weren't hurt."

"You and me both."

Ben stepped away from me and went over to the officers. He spoke to them at length, though I couldn't hear what was being said. A paramedic took me to the ambulance and checked my blood pressure and vitals. When Ben returned, he said,

"They're going to file the report. I'm going to take you home."

Now that I was out of imminent danger, my body betrayed me. My teeth chattered, and I felt cold even though the night was muggy. Ben put one hand at the small of my back and guided me to his car. Bo came along and hopped up on my lap once I was in. Ben laughed—the first time I ever heard him laugh, I thought. "He thinks he's a lap dog."

I smiled and leaned my face down against Bo's neck. I was able to give Ben directions, even though I felt dazed. When we pulled up to my building, he said, "Let me walk you up."

I shook my head. "Please just let me go up alone."

He nodded but didn't ask me any questions. "Call my cell phone when you are in and safe."

I agreed, grabbed Bo's leash and went up to my apartment. When I walked in, David stood up, the anger gone from his face and replaced by his usual serene appearance—albeit a little worried.

"One minute," I told him. I picked up the phone and dialed Ben's number. "I'm in and okay."

"Good. Tomorrow we interview Daniel after work. I'll come to the lab to get you."

"Thanks."

I hung up, then turned to face David. "I was attacked. By the killer—or at least the person who's left me the souvenirs. Bo saved my life."

"Oh, my God," he rushed over and wrapped his arms around me, then bent down to pat Bo. He stood up again and grabbed me in a bear hug. "It's all my fault. I shouldn't have said what I did. I don't want to fight, Billie. Please…you've got to be careful."

"I know. He slipped away. But…" I lifted my head and gave a halfhearted smile. "There is one good thing. Bo got a piece of him. Literally. Bo bit him, tore his pant leg, and now we have his blood. We have his DNA."

"That's good news. So then the police can catch him."

"Well, only if he's in the system. But it's evidence. Little by little I'm wrapping a noose around his neck."

"Well, darling, let's just hope he doesn't wrap one around yours first." David leaned in and kissed my neck. "I'm sorry about everything." He kissed my lips.

"I'm sorry, too."

"Now will you let Tommy Salami be your bodyguard?"

"Unfortunately, David, I don't think I have much choice. As soon as my father hears about tonight, Tommy will be on my doorstep."

Chapter 15

Ben called Lewis about what happened that night. Lewis called Mikey. Mikey called Dad. Dad called Tommy Salami.

And the next morning, when I rose predawn for work, Tommy Salami was waiting for me, sitting on the trunk of my car with a huge bag of McDonald's and two extra-large coffees.

"Egg McMuffin?"

"You know I don't eat that crap. And you

were supposed to lay off it. What about your cholesterol?"

"Eh…I take my Lipitor. I can eat eggs."

"Whatever," I smiled at him. "Believe it or not, Tommy, it's good to see you."

"You know you shouldn't drive on your spare tire. It's a piece of shit. While you're in the lab today, I'll take it to get new tires. I checked out the treads. I think you can use a new left-front tire, too."

I rolled my eyes. As the only daughter of Frank Quinn, I was used to all the guys in my life being overprotective pit bulls.

"Fine," I said.

"And your father wants to know when the last time you changed the oil was."

"Go ahead and get it changed."

"Billie, you have to stay on top of routine maintenance."

"This from a man who takes Lipitor so he can eat a dozen McMuffins each morning. How about a little maintenance on your health?"

"You know I can't resist the golden arches, Billie."

"Fine, you big lug, let's go."

I climbed into the driver's seat. Tommy Salami

easily weighed two hundred and eighty pounds.
Most of it was muscle. He worked out each day,
lifting weights, a regime he perfected during the
four years he served for breaking and entering,
with an assault charge thrown in for good
measure. During the Suicide King case, he had
been shot protecting me. My father treated him
like another son since then, and I was fond of
Tommy. But he reminded me of Bo—untrained
and a little overgrown.

"I'd rather you let me drive, Billie," he said,
climbing into the passenger seat.

"I know that, Tommy, just as you know there's
no way I'm letting you drive, so let's resume our
little relationship the way it works for us, okay?"

"Okay, but if your father asks, you tell him you
let me drive."

"Fine."

I pulled out into the road, checking my
rearview mirror. I was in full paranoia mode.
Seeing I wasn't being followed, I headed for the
Jersey Turnpike and then the lab.

I pulled into the parking garage and found a
space on the second story.

"Now you know the drill, Tommy. Only I'm

allowed in the lab. So…you can get the tires changed, the oil checked, and you can take a long lunch—I promise I'll eat at my desk."

"What time we going home tonight?"

"After work Ben Sato is coming to get me. He's a detective. We have something to do. You can follow us, and then after that, we'll go home."

"What about dinner?"

Tommy liked his three squares.

"I'll treat. How about that Italian place you like in Paramus?"

"Sounds good to me, Billie. Now you be careful."

I winked at him as I climbed out of the car. "You, too."

We locked eyes for a minute. I looked away first, welling up. Not many people will risk their life for you.

I walked out of the garage and into the lab, showing my badge. Lewis was in early, of course— he had beaten me by ten minutes according to the log at the security desk.

"Hey, Lewis," I popped my head into his office. "All in one piece?"

I nodded.

"Billie…sit down."

"Please, no lectures. I know this is dangerous, but I'm so close. I know I am."

"You're so close because he's decided to target you. The publicity from the Justice Foundation has put him over the edge. He hungers for infamy, for immortality. Think of how infamous he would be if he got to you, Billie. Your mother, then you all these years later."

"I'm going to catch him first."

Lewis shook his head. "I think you should go into protective custody until we process all the DNA we have related to this and see if we have a match."

"Who put you up to this?"

"No one."

"No…that's not you. Who told you to talk to me? My dad?"

Lewis sighed. "Ben."

I felt betrayed. "Why?"

"He thinks this guy won't rest until he's killed you. And his boldness—the attack in the vestibule out where he could have been seen or caught—means he's not playing this cold and calculating. He's taking risks. And that signals trouble. He's not in control anymore. His demons are controlling him."

"No protective custody. I came to work with Tommy Salami."

"And no elaborate ruses to ditch him? You'll let him guard you?"

I nodded. "I'll be a good little girl."

Lewis smiled wanly.

"You look even more morose than usual," I said.

"Still nothing from C.C."

"Lewis, you know, this isn't something you can control, like the lab and its specimens. It's the human heart, the single most unpredictable thing in the world."

"I know…. Speaking of which, Joe and Vanessa are going to a major political fund-raiser tonight. Black tie at the Waldorf Astoria. Rubbing elbows with blue-bloods. What in God's name does he see in her?"

"She's beautiful but so transparent. How could our guy fall for her?" I concurred.

"I can't stand it. And now that Marcus Hopkins was exonerated, he's more famous than ever. He's the go-to guy for celebrities now. Instead of Justice Foundation cases, he's being inundated by celebrities gone wild who got themselves in a jam. Shoplifting actresses, buttocks-grabbing B-listers."

I shook my head and got up from the chair. "This is all giving me a headache. I've got a lot of rape kits to process today. Talk to you later."

The day flew by. When we get the films back of DNA, it looks almost like key-punch cards. In general, at a crime scene, we take DNA from the victim. But then we also collect DNA from the people closest to the victim. It would only make sense, for instance, that a mother would have the DNA of her children and husband on her and around her. If we collect hair fibers, it is only logical that the hairs of all the people in the house would be scattered on carpets, on bed sheets and in the bathroom sink.

If we're lucky, however, the culprit will also have left some of his DNA scattered about. Those samples that do not match the victim or any members of the victim's household are the samples we come to believe belonged to the rapist or murderer. When the films come back, the key-punch-looking samples don't line up in the same places as the known persons. That unknown key-punch, that unknown human bar code…that's our guy.

I worked straight through lunch, stopping for

a visit to the snack machine, where Cheez-Its and a cup of coffee constituted my meal. I lived a coffee-fueled existence, occasionally swearing off caffeine, only to come back to it, like a cast-off lover pleading to be let back into her partner's bed.

Around six, security called and told me Ben Sato was there. I felt my heart lift for a moment, and then shook my head. Something about him connected us. I supposed, like David, like Lewis, a shared hint of melancholy. A shared existence like Achlys. In Lewis's case, his first love was murdered and her body hidden in the bayou. He left academia for work in the crime lab and never looked back.

I phoned David. "I'm going to interview my mother's former boyfriend tonight. Then I'm collecting DNA from my dad's house. I won't be home until late."

"Does your father know?"

"No. I can't bring myself to tell him. I suppose that makes me a terrible daughter."

"No. It just makes you a daughter determined to find her mother's killer, no matter where the truth leads you."

"What are you up to?"

"Well, the news has broken about Tony Castle. I'm here in the Justice Foundation's offices. The phones are ringing off the hook and there are press people camping out on the sidewalk."

"Great. Just what I need. More of my name and face making the papers."

"Exactly. You be extra careful."

"I will."

"Billie?"

"Hmm?"

"Are you going to interview this guy with Ben Sato?"

I hesitated. "Ye-es."

I held my breath waiting for David to get angry or mistrusting again.

"Good. I want someone there with you, and if it can't be me, it should be him. Listen, Billie…I had a moment of jealousy. You're my girl. You know," he lowered his voice, I guess so no one there would overhear him. "Every time we make love, those first seconds when I slide inside you my soul leaves me. I love you, and I'm sorry I acted the way I did."

"It's okay. And for the record, when you first go inside me, I feel that way, too."

I hung up the phone, smiling to myself. After saying good-night to Lewis, I went to the lobby where Ben waited for me, wearing a dark suit expertly tailored to his physique. He gave a small bow, and I bowed back.

"Come. I'll drive."

"I have a bodyguard today. I need to have him follow us. He won't get in the way." At least I hoped he wouldn't.

Ben smiled. "Good. I was thinking perhaps I would have to guard you."

I thought of telling him I didn't appreciate his suggestion to Lewis that I needed protective custody, but decided not to. Maybe after what he shared about his sister, it seemed like a chivalrous gesture to me.

Ben followed me to the parking garage. I noticed his walk was very fluid. For his size he moved gracefully. On the other hand, Mr. Salami was anything but graceful. When we got to my car, Tommy was waiting, leaning against the trunk.

"Look, Billie…got it washed and waxed, too."

My Cadillac did shine.

"Thanks, Tommy. This is Detective Ben Sato." Tommy looked like a scared little boy.

"Don't worry, Tommy. He's happy you're watching over me. He's not interested in your record."

At that, Tommy visibly relaxed and shook Ben's hand.

"Listen, Tommy, we have to go to Ridgewood. Do you want to meet me at the Italian place? I could have Ben drop me off."

"I'm supposed to stick to you like glue. Those were your father's exact words."

"I know," I said gently, "but I have a real, live police detective with me, so it would be all right if we simply met at the restaurant. Go shop at the mall or something. I'll meet you there at eight. Okay? No sense you following us just to sit outside while we interview a potential witness."

Cautiously he said, "Okay. But if your father asks, I never left your side."

"Fine."

Tommy got behind the wheel of my car and drove away, and Ben and I got into his Acura and headed toward Ridgewood to visit Daniel Carter. Ben had phoned him about a "police matter," and we were scheduled to meet him at his office.

Ridgewood is a rather Currier & Ives kind of

town, picturesque, with a main street of little quaint shops. We found the Carter Professional Plaza and then Daniel's office.

Ben and I entered. The lobby area was tasteful and elegant, but not opulent, with very thick carpeting in a blue the color of a Delft plate, and antique reproductions. In one corner stood a tall display cabinet filled with miniature tall ships, all hand carved with astounding detail down to the little portholes and ropes and life rafts. Next to each ship was a completion date: *Lady Hawke*, Daniel Carter, completed May 1997.

"Amazing," I whispered.

Ben bent down to look more closely at one. "Talented man."

A receptionist entered the waiting area.

"I'm sorry, I stepped out to freshen up. Are you Detective Sato?" she asked Ben.

"Yes."

"Mr. Carter's expecting you. Office over there in the corner," she gestured. "Good night."

Ben and I said good-night and went and rapped softly on Daniel's office door.

"Come on in," came a voice on the other side.

We entered the impressive corner office. The

furnishings were antique, and an immense saltwater tank took up one entire wall.

"Mr. Carter," Ben stuck out his hand.

"Sit down. Now, I have to say I'm very curious why exactly you're here."

"This is Billie Quinn." Ben waited for the recognition to cross Daniel's face. It did in an instant.

"My God, you look just like Claire."

"Thank you," I said softly.

"Some developments have occurred with respect to the investigation into Mrs. Quinn's death. We were hoping to interview you."

"Anything." He gestured toward two chairs. Like my father, Daniel Carter was still very attractive, probably around fifty-five. He was sandy blond, with the tan of a man who got to golf frequently— or sail, judging by his hobby. His eyes were hazel, and he had a small cleft in his chin. I watched Daniel for any hint of guilt. There was none that I could see.

"Tell me about your relationship with her," Ben said.

"She was the love of my life. After we broke up, I eventually married, you know. Twice, in fact. But it never worked out. I wouldn't have traded my marriages. I'm still good friends with my first wife, and my second wife gave me a wonderful son—Brendan. He's at Yale. But Claire was the one. I used to think perhaps I just recalled her so perfectly because she was my first love, but really, there was something extraordinary about her. Smart as a whip, funny, charming, but so humble, so caring. We dated exclusively for a long time, and I just couldn't get my nerve up to ask her to marry me. Marriage seemed so huge at twenty-two. Huge. Then she met Frank, and…they were married in a very short time. My eternal loss."

"Did that upset you?" Ben asked.

"Of course. Not anger, though. I was sad for a long, long time. I just…was sad. But you know, time heals. I moved on. We'd keep in touch from time to time. Exchange Christmas cards. I ran into her occasionally—once my father was having open-heart surgery in the same hospital as Frank's mother. Just one of those weird coincidences. We ran into each other in the hospital gift shop. We decided to grab some coffee in the cafeteria. We caught up. She showed me pictures of you." He looked at me. "God, it's uncanny."

"And then how did you hear about her murder?"

"I heard about her disappearance first. I knew it was foul play. I knew Claire. She was so responsible. She just wasn't the type to walk away from her life. I phoned the police and told them just that, but the lead detective, he was not overly receptive."

Ben nodded, encouraging Daniel to go on.

"Then, of course, they found her, God rest her soul. I went to the funeral. I was married by then, but I took it very, very hard. I offered your father my condolences, Billie. I could see how torn up he was."

"Is there anything at all you can remember that might help us?" I asked.

"I would lie awake nights going over every conversation, every nuance, but nothing. Nothing came to me then. Or now."

"What about the name Andrew? Does it mean anything to you?"

He looked like he was struggling to remember something.

"Another boyfriend, maybe?" I asked him.

He shook his head. "No. But…something. Give me a minute." He leaned back in his immense leather chair and pressed his index fingers to his temples and rubbed in a circular motion, in deep thought.

"You know, I think there was someone who had a crush on her. She told me. I mean, it was from when we were still together, maybe. Made her uncomfortable. But for the life of me, I can't recall."

"Did you mention it to the police?"

He shook his head. "It was…like a schoolboy crush. But hearing the name, I do recall her one time saying he…what was it? Had some fairy-tale dream of marrying her. I took it to be a childish thing. Like some kid from the Sunday school class she taught at St. Joan's before she had you kids. Like I said, it was a while ago. But—"

"What?" I leaned forward in my seat.

"I…think she may have been afraid."

"Thank you, Mr. Carter. Thank you," I breathed out. This was something. A sliver of something.

"Have I helped?"

"A little. It all helps. It's like putting together a giant jigsaw puzzle."

"Can I tell you one story about her?"

"I'd love it." I leaned forward a little. Tidbits about my mother were rare.

"Well…I was going through my first divorce. I ran into her at the Paramus Park Mall. She was pregnant with you, and she had your brother in a stroller. And I was there buying a Valentine's gift for the woman who would be my second wife. I was still wistful for your mother. I had her up on a pedestal. And she smiled at me and said something very wise. 'Daniel, you think you love me with all your heart, but when you have children, you will understand what it means to love with all your being.' Billie…you and your brother were her soul. She loved your father—much to my chagrin." He smiled. "But you were her soul."

I smiled at him. "I can see why she loved you." I looked over at Ben.

"Thank you for your time." Ben stood, gave a small bow and turned to leave.

"Thank you," I said to Daniel. "I really appreciate it."

Ben left the office leaving me alone with Daniel.

"You know, Billie…I can't claim that I suffered from her death a fraction of your family's suffering, but I don't know as I ever got over the thought of her last hours being horrible like that. Hope you get the bastard."

"Thanks."

I left his office and met Ben in the lobby, where he was waiting. He didn't say anything until we climbed in his car.

"We need to get your father's DNA."

"I don't want him to know. It would break his heart. Let's drive by his house and see if he's home. I have the key. I can sneak in and get his toothbrush, or something else."

"Good. Let's go."

I tried to quell the guilty feeling in my stomach. How could I be doing this to my dad, the man who taught me to tie my shoes, who taught me to swing the bat at t-ball?

I gave Ben directions. I noticed he was even more silent than usual.

"What are you thinking?"

"That's a very American habit."

"What is?"

"Wanting to know someone else's thoughts."

I didn't reply.

"I think the answer is in front of us, but we just don't see it yet."

A short time later I instructed him to turn off the main road, and through a series of left and right turns we ended up in front of my father's darkened house. He wasn't home. But I was convinced I would soon be rousing old ghosts.

Chapter 16

"Wait in the car," I told Ben. I let myself into Dad's house with a key, but didn't turn on the lights. I didn't want the neighbors to see a strange car in the driveway and tell him someone had been there. I let my eyes adjust to the darkness. He always keeps a small lamp lit on a desk in the den, so the place was dim but not pitch-black. The stairs were directly in front of me, and I took them one at a time to the second-floor landing. Once there, I turned on the hall light and moved down to the master bedroom.

After Mom died, he hadn't changed much about our house. He still had a king-size bed with a white chenille bedspread, an oak dresser and two oak night stands. They were heavy pieces of furniture and had belonged to my maternal grandparents. Pictures throughout the room were of Mom, Mikey and me. I walked over to his dresser.

I guess you can tell a lot about a man by what he keeps on his dresser. David keeps a copy of the first-edition Camus I gave him, and a photo of me and Bo. My dad had a small crystal dish where he kept his keys and change. Next to it was a wooden box. I lifted its lid and inside were my baby teeth and locks of hair from my first haircut, Mikey's baby shoe and photos of my mom. I closed the box.

Next to it, in a five-by-seven frame stood a photo of my mother holding me in my christening dress, and next to it was a smaller photo of her on her wedding day. Next to that picture was one of Mikey and her on his first day of kindergarten. My eyes grew moist. I looked away. A wood and pewter crucifix hung on the wall next to the door to the bathroom. I needed to get his toothbrush and just leave.

I walked into the blue-and-white-tiled bathroom, which overlooked the backyard and turned on the light. There, resting in the toothbrush stand, was my dad's toothbrush. I took it out and felt another tidal wave of guilt swamp me. He would wonder what happened to his toothbrush, wonder how he could have misplaced it. I despised the subterfuge, but I knew if he thought I doubted him, doubted who my father was, I would break his heart.

I shut off the bathroom light. Looking out in the backyard, a silvery sliver of moon hung in the sky. I blinked hard twice. I thought I saw a flashlight in my old treehouse. I looked closer, and I was positive someone was in the treehouse, a ramshackle old thing built of plywood and two-by-fours by Mikey and me the summer I turned eleven.

I fled from the bathroom and took the stairs two at a time. I ran out the front door, which locked behind me, and raced to the car.

"Ben," I said, leaning through the passenger window—it was a hot night and he had the windows rolled down. "Someone's in the backyard." I put the toothbrush on the passenger seat as he climbed out.

"Stay here!" he commanded.

"Not on your life." I took off in the direction of my old treehouse. Ben wasn't far behind me—but I did have a head start on him—and I knew where the treehouse was in the yard. I could have found it blindfolded.

As I neared the treehouse, I could see someone jump down from it.

"Freeze!" I shouted, running faster. My lungs felt like they were bursting, and I started sweating right away in the heat.

The figure, dressed in dark clothes, ran toward the woods. I dashed after him, the underbrush scratching my face and tugging at my pant legs.

My childhood neighborhood is set up with about forty houses backing up to woods, beyond them is a Little League field, and past that is a chain link fence. Beyond that is a horse farm and riding ring. My parents chose it for its bucolic setting but convenience to highways. The woods are dense, and because it was summer, everything was in full bloom, lush, and prickers and sharp leaves clawed at my clothes and hair.

I could hear the man ahead of me—his breathing. I could hear us all crashing through the brush. I held my arms in front of me, feeling like I was running completely blind, but having no choice. Behind me, I heard Ben stumbling through the woods, just like me, grunts and exhales as he pushed through leaves and branches.

"Police! Freeze!" he shouted. "Freeze!"

But the dark-clothed figure ran on. Eventually, the man got to the Little League field. He seemed to get an inhuman burst of energy, and he sprinted across the field and bolted toward the fence, starting to scale it like Spider Man. I ran as hard as I could, turning back once in time to see Ben stumble on a large tree bough.

I raced on. Ben called out to me, "I'm calling for backup. Let him go."

But I thought this might be my one chance. Ignoring Ben, I sprinted as hard as I could, scaling the fence and managing to grasp the very bottom of the toe of his shoe. He kicked my fingers into the chain-link fence—I felt like he broke them—and then threw one leg, then the other, over the fence. He dropped down and took off toward the horse farm. I got to the top, then fell on the other side with a loud thud. My shoulder registered pain, and I wondered if I had dislocated it.

I rolled over and very slowly stood back up again, shaking my head as if dazed. I could barely make out the man running across the horse field. I couldn't let him go.

"Shit!" I cursed. I started sprinting toward the horse farm. The barn doors were unlocked and I entered the stable. I could hear the horses were agitated. One was rising up on its hind legs in his stall. I heard someone moving around in the hay in the loft.

"Come out, you bastard!" I shouted up at the rafters.

I ran over to the ladder that went up to the loft. I wasn't keen on being at a disadvantage—the person on the second floor of a stairwell is always in a better position than the person ascending the stairs. Still, with Ben and backup coming soon, I was less afraid. I started up the ladder and could see him moving toward the open end of the loft.

"Stay right there," I warned him as I reached the loft.

He looked back at me. No mask, but his face was obscured by the sweatshirt hood he wore.

Then he calmly leaped off the edge of the loft and into the hay of the stall below.

I ran toward the edge. He was unhurt, and I wanted to chase him as I saw him get up and head out the barn door, but I was already aching from my fall from the fence.

I ran back to the ladder and started downward. When I reached the bottom, Ben was there.

"Any sign of him?" I asked him in between gasps for breath from the exertion and pain.

He shook his head. "He's amazingly athletic."

"I know." I was panting.

"You're hurt."

I nodded.

"Where?"

"Shoulder, mostly."

He rubbed his hands together and looked intently at them. Then, without another word, he laid his hands on my shoulder. I felt intense warmth. He manipulated my shoulder a bit, and the pain left me.

"What'd you do?"

He just smiled mysteriously at me. "Secret."

I rotated my arm and shoulder. "It feels okay."

"Good."

Backup didn't arrive for five more minutes. He had called for backup to the Little League field, and one car had arrived—but then hadn't thought to come to the barn and riding ring.

Ben told the two officers what happened, but it was no use. Our suspect was long gone. The cops dropped us back off at Ben's car, and we climbed in. I put the toothbrush in an evidence bag, and Ben took me to Paramus where I still had to meet Tommy Salami.

"Thanks, Ben." I smiled at him as I got out of the car.

"You were a warrior today," he said.

"So were you."

My car was in the parking lot, so I assumed Tommy was there. I waved goodbye to Ben and then walked inside. Tommy was waiting at the bar.

"What happened to you?" he asked, pulling a piece of hay from my hair.

"Don't ask."

"Why?"

"Because that way, if my father asks you any questions, you can play dumb."

"Sounds like a plan. I don't like lying—too much to remember. I always screw it up."

"Well then, let's just eat dinner and we won't tell him anything."

Tommy and I were seated at a table. But even though I ate and drank wine, I was replaying the night and feeling seriously unnerved. I talked with Tommy, but my mind was already drifting to the world of genetic bar codes. What would my own DNA show when compared with Frank Quinn's? And who was so interested in me and my family?

Chapter 17

"Open wide." The next morning, at 7:00 a.m., Lewis stood next to me ready to take a swab sample of the inside of my cheek for the DNA testing. I dutifully opened my mouth.

After Lewis was finished, he labeled everything. The lab was silent, and as usual it was just the two of us.

"Wilhelmina, I have something to say."

"I know what it is."

"You do not."

"Lewis, believe it or not, in some sick twist of fate, we appear to be twins separated at birth. I mean, no swab would declare us twins, but I know what you're going to say and do before you even open your mouth. And you can finish my sentences."

"Well, I'm going to speak my mind anyway."

"How uncharacteristically bold of you."

"Billie, why are you running this test?"

"Because there are rumors that my mother was having an affair. Because there are rumors I might not even be my father's child. And if I'm not, then that opens up my mother's murder to a whole new theory. I have to know. Why sign that one letter 'Daddy'?"

"To mess with you. And beyond that, DNA isn't parentage."

"What the hell are you talking about? You're the leading DNA expert in the friggin' country, Lewis. DNA is everything."

"No. I'm telling you I've been mistaken all these years."

I stared at Lewis. I had never, ever known him to say he made a mistake. Our lab, *his* lab, didn't make them. He didn't tolerate them. Sloppy lab work or field work was the fastest way to get fired at our lab. That's why new forensics graduates from across the country flooded us with résumés. They wanted to work for the best. They wanted to work for Lewis LeBarge.

"You don't make mistakes," I said evenly.

"I do."

I exhaled. "What are you talking about, Lewis?"

"Billie…when I hired you, I heard…might as well tell you, from Morris Cheswick, who your father was."

Morris was this absolutely anal Ph.D. criminalist who was in line for my job before I got it.

"And?" I arched an eyebrow. This was the first I ever heard of this.

"And I decided, out of pure curiosity, that I would interview you. I mean, your academic credentials were impeccable. Your work experience stellar. You were brilliant—that much was obvious. Your letters of recommendation were glowing. All the things I like to see—driven, intense, meticulous, genius. But I had no intention of giving you the job. A daughter of a known felon working in a crime lab. The idea is laughable. And then I met you."

I recalled my interview. He was maddeningly obtuse and acted bemused the whole time.

"And I decided, dear Wilhelmina, that I would far more prefer to come in at 7:00 a.m. to your sardonic sense of humor and your beauty and charm and charisma, than to come in and face the boring Morris Cheswick. You were smarter and better qualified, anyway."

"So what does this have to do with the swab you just took?"

"Well, then we became friends. You tolerated my penchant for blood-spatter patterns, and I tolerated your habit of occasionally showing up with Tommy Salami. Then you took me to meet your family. Remember? I couldn't get back to New Orleans that Christmas—too much of a backlog at the lab to take the week off. You felt sorry for me."

I nodded. "I remember."

"I tried to kiss you under the mistletoe, but you told me we were better off as friends. I acted hurt, you snapped at me to get over it. And then your brother came and talked me into doing shots called Angel's Nipples. Only he used a cruder term for the anatomical part."

"Oh, yeah. What? Sambuca and Baileys? I don't even remember."

"Neither do I. Frankly, I barely remember the night, but after that, I was officially adopted by your family."

"Yes, you're our long-lost New Orleans brother with the tarantula and brain fetish."

"Billie…one thing I've learned is your family loves you as much as it's possible for one human being to love another. And even if that swab there says something else in terms of the little spiral ladders of the human genome, you are a Quinn and your daddy couldn't love you any more."

My eyes welled a little. "But, Lewis…"

"No, Billie. Is it worth finding out? Frank Quinn is your father. Michael Quinn is your brother. DNA be damned, Billie. That's reality. Do you really want to know?"

"Yes." I turned around and left his office before he could see me cry. I did want to know. It wasn't that his logic didn't make sense. It did. But I still needed to know. I had learned, over the years, that I shared something with children of people who committed suicide, people whose parents are murdered. The specter of the event cast a long shadow, years and years after the murder, after the death. It colored everything about my life.

When I got to my desk, I saw the framed picture of Mikey and me and my dad from game six of the Mets versus Boston Red Sox game. We had won. What was it, 1987? I remembered that the game had been rained out once, and when it took place the next night, it had been unseasonably chilly with a cold, steady, wet drizzle. And in the euphoria of New York celebrating the sheer joy of winning the series, we hadn't even noticed how cold we were.

We had cheered and shrieked and danced. We rode the train from the stadium into Manhattan and made our way to Times Square. This was before Disney brought *Beauty and the Beast* and the aura of cleanliness to Times Square. Back then, it was still pawn shops and a few peep shows. But mostly I remember cabbies stopping right there in the middle of the street and getting out and dancing in the sheer jubilance of a city celebrating.

At some point, a cabbie hugged me and Mikey and we were all screaming, "Number One! Number One!" I asked the cabbie to take a picture of Mikey and me and Dad, and he obliged. And that picture, the joy of the night on our faces, sat in a silver frame.

I looked at my computer. Not yet seven-thirty in the morning. I picked up my phone and dialed Mikey.

"Hello?" he answered, his voice croaking.

"Did I wake you?" Of course I had.

"What's up?" I could sense he was waking himself, worried.

"Nothing. I just wanted to hear your voice."

"Baby? What's going on? You and David have a fight?"

"No."

"What, then? I hear it."

"Nothing," I insisted.

"Billie, I'm the guy who used to catch tadpoles and put them in your apple juice glass in the morning. You can't bullshit me."

I was silent. Why had I called him?

"Mikey?"

"Yeah?"

"Will you love me always? No matter what? My brother until the day I die?"

"Billie," his voice was soothing. "Ain't nothing you can do to chase me away. I'd take a bullet for you, and nothing will ever change that. You want me to come meet you somewhere?"

"No. I just needed to hear that."

"Billie…I know I'm sometimes more trouble than I'm worth. I know it's broken your heart when I'm in jail and I make you worry. But you gotta know that I love you so much it hurts. You're my sister, yeah, but…you know I don't like to talk about this shit."

"I know."

"So I'll just say it. I was there that night with you, Billie. I was there. I was there when we went to school and the kids stared at us because our mom disappeared. I beat up that boy who teased you about it that time. It goes beyond brother and sister. We're one heart. We're like twins."

Twins. If only our DNA would show that.

"Thanks. I just needed to hear that."

"Love you, brat."

"Love you, too."

I hung up the phone. What would happen to Mikey and me if it turned out we had different fathers? I didn't even want to think about it. I risked not only breaking my heart, but my father's and Mikey's.

I lifted a model of a spiral of a gene from my desk. It was plastic and colorful, a giveaway paperweight from a company that made the swabs we used for testing. It twisted and spiraled looking a little like a ladder made of licorice that's been twirled around.

Scientists were mapping out the human genome even as I toiled in the lab. Each day brought advances in understanding of who we were as humans. Because of the work Lewis and I did, we tended to believe humans were what their genetic destiny created them to be.

Nature or nurture. I suppose I was about to find out.

Chapter 18

A couple of days passed. Ben Sato called me a few times to see how my DNA tests were going, and I told him that as soon as I had the results he would be the first to know. I tried to busy myself. At night I played Scrabble with David or read voraciously. One evening David and I went to Quinn's to play darts.

I tried to keep my mind off my attacker, but it was hard not to feel as if his eyes were on me every time I left my apartment. I willed the DNA tests to be completed faster, but nothing about this was in my control. Science is like a cold-hearted lover. It will leave you brokenhearted. It's not like a jury, swayed by emotion. Eyewitnesses don't matter—they're unreliable anyway. DNA is the genetic code. Unbreakable.

Lewis approached me on a Friday. The same day the weather broke. Actually, the weather did more than break. It poured. The rain seemed like the proverbial Great Flood, and weathermen and radio DJs were regularly making jokes about building an ark. That morning, Tommy Salami and I decided he should stay home. No need to have us both drowning like wet rats. Of course, he gave me his usual, "Don't tell your father," like the two of us were truant grade-schoolers. David walked me down to my car, holding a big golf umbrella over my head. I climbed in my car, shook off the cold droplets of water and drove to the lab.

I walked into the lab around six-forty-five, shaking my hair, and opting for a ponytail to contain my wet mop head. I actually felt chilly for the first time in ages and went in search of a brewing coffee pot. Lewis found me as I was stirring my mug.

"Got the DNA results on some of your samples."

"And?"

"Come to my office."

I didn't like the sound of that. When we got there, I shut the door behind me, my knees actually feeling weak, and collapsed into one of the velour chairs facing his desk.

"First off, your paternity test." He slid a file folder across the desk. I leaned forward and read the results.

I was a hundred percent Quinn. My father's daughter.

"Oh, Lewis," I smiled through tears. I shut the folder and clutched it to my chest and actually gave it a hug.

"Yes, you are absolutely related to that motley crew—genetically and, quite frankly, with that attitude of yours." He grinned at me. "I'm honestly pleased, Billie. Wouldn't seem right after all these years for you to find out Frank isn't your dad."

"Thanks, Lewis."

"More information." He slid another file folder across the desk.

I opened the folder. The flecks of dried blood on the lock of hair left for me on my car that night were *also* a match for me. It was my mother's hair. Without any doubt, this wasn't a hoax. My mother's killer had resurfaced for sure.

"Seems like that bit of news matches the weather. Downright gloomy," he drawled. "You know, every time I see rain like this it reminds me of New Orleans drowning. I swear I almost put a shot of bourbon in my coffee today."

I kept staring at the results. "Lewis, all this time, I had some vague hope she hadn't suffered. I pictured a bloodless death. Quick. No torture. Every time my mind would go that way, I would stop it in its tracks. Especially with this place. You can go nuts thinking about how people died."

"I know. It's easier when it's all test tubes, and you don't think much beyond X and Y chromosomes to how and why someone was murdered."

"Exactly. But the blood on that lock of hair, it means she suffered, Lewis. And I've known it. I've known it all along, but it still, well, it makes me want to stick a shot of bourbon in my coffee today, too."

"Why don't you take the rest of the day off?"

"Nah." I shook my head. "I have that new guy starting—Antoine Purcell. He's just a kid. Smart as hell, though. His transcripts—perfect 4.0."

"Another scholar. Excellent."

"You should see his handwriting, though." I laughed. "He should have been a doctor. Unreadable. Writes like a sixth-grader."

And then it hit me.

"Oh, God, Lewis…"

"What?"

I stood up. "I have to run home. I'll be back before nine—maybe a few minutes later with traffic."

"What? You're disturbing me."

"You're already disturbed. I just have to get something."

I didn't have time to explain. I grabbed my commuter mug from his desk and hurried from his office and then the lab. I raced to my car.

A clue had been there in front of me the whole time. The cards from the box my father gave me.

Of course.

Andrew…was a child.

Chapter 19

Back at my apartment, I kissed David as he rolled over in bed and stretched.

"Didn't I walk you downstairs at like five-thirty?"

I nodded. "I forgot something."

"And you drove all the way back here? I could have brought it to you, honey."

"No. I needed to come home. By the way, the DNA tests? I'm all Quinn."

"That's great news." He leaned up on one elbow. "You look gorgeous today."

I stared at him. "I'm soaking wet."

"I like the wet T-shirt look." His smile was playful yet seductive.

"Well, no time for a quickie today. I've got to get back to the lab." I pulled the box of my mother's things down from the closet and pulled out the cards from Andrew.

Opening one, I looked at the handwriting again. I showed it to David.

"What does this say to you…? The handwriting."

"Looks like my handwriting when I was in junior high."

"I'm not wrong, then." I didn't need a handwriting expert to tell me what was right there. "Thanks, sweetie." I leaned down and kissed him passionately on the mouth. Then I hurried to the kitchen and pulled out a gallon Ziploc bag. I didn't want to risk my evidence getting wet. With the cards secure, I pulled a sweater off of the brass coatrack next to the apartment door. I put it on under my raincoat and then bolted, calling out, "Bye, David," as I slammed the door.

Safely in my Cadillac, I pulled out into morning rush hour feeling optimistic. I drove back to the lab and hurried in to see Lewis. Just as I had with David, I opened a card and showed it to him.

"What does this say to you?"

"Some little high school boy has a major crush on you."

"Not me. Look at the name."

"Claire. Your mother."

I nodded. "When Ben and I interviewed Daniel, he said something about her being a little…unnerved—I don't think he used that word—but something he couldn't put his finger on, by someone with a crush on her. I think Andrew—whoever he is—is the killer. And I think she was his first victim. But not his last. So all we have to do is figure out who he is, and then track him through time. And we solve the case."

"How were the cards stored?"

"In a box with other stuff my mom saved. And these cards were all separate—saved with her most prized possessions—cards from me and Mikey and my dad. She was worried about these cards, Lewis. Keeping them to show my dad or the police. I just feel it."

"The box was kept dry all these years?"

"In Dad's closet."

"Then maybe we have his saliva. We can try to get a sample from here, where he licked it. It's a long shot—a lot of years have passed. But," he lifted the envelope to his nose. "I don't smell mildew or dampness. Let's try it."

"Great. And if we get a DNA sample, then we can try to match it against the scrap of pant leg and blood that Bo managed to get. I also want to try something else."

"What?"

"Hypnosis."

"Here, follow this pen with your eyes. You are getting sleepy...very sleepy. When I count to ten, you will give Lewis LeBarge all your money. In cash."

"Don't be such an idiot. Look, I'm a witness. And maybe somewhere in my brain is the answer."

"Billie, you have been over that night in so much detail, I think you've literally relived every breath you took then."

I shook my head. "I want to try. You're a scientist. You know the brain stores far more than we ever access."

"I had a friend who was at the forefront of

studies involving MDMA before the government shut him down."

MDMA was a drug some thought helped a person recall suppressed memories, or memories in greater detail.

"And?"

"And he used it himself a few times. He was ten years older than I was. A product of the late sixties. Timothy Leary. Dropping acid. He said he was able to recall the exact angle of the pile carpeting in his child mind when he would lie on the floor watching television. He could recall specific dust bunnies. It's all in the brain, but we process things so we don't overload. The brain decides what's necessary to recall and what can be tucked away in some dusty old file."

"Exactly. Maybe I've been trying so hard that my brain just shut down. Locked away a secret."

"What does Ben think?"

"I don't know. Why does it matter what he thinks?"

"I know you love David. I know you adore him." He twirled a pencil in his hand. "But you have some kind of connection with Ben."

"We barely know each other."

"Don't get defensive. I didn't say you would act on it. It's just there. Something. A deep and quiet passion for what you do. Maybe in some Jungian sense, he's your other half. The warrior and the scientific mind, both doing battle against evil. I don't know."

"You're definitely drinking too much while pondering Greek mythology."

"I'm just saying. Ben will know whether it's a good idea or not. You know, Tommy Two Trees said to me that Ben Sato was the man he respected most in law enforcement. As he put it, it was as if he was born to instinctively do this."

"Maybe… You win. We'll ask him what he thinks."

"Good. Don't want to do anything to screw up that brain of yours. I need it too much around here."

When I had a quiet moment later on, I called Ben's cell phone and explained what I wanted to do.

"Have you ever been hypnotized before?"

"No."

"You might not be suggestible. A lot of people aren't. Academic types especially."

"Because they resist. Lord knows I've never done drugs in my life precisely because my brain was always going a million miles an hour and I didn't want to mess with it. It's a control thing. But I *want* to be hypnotized. Don't you think it's at least worth a try given some of these new clues?" I had told him about the DNA, about my gut feeling.

"I'll arrange it. The department's psychologist can do it."

"Fine. The sooner the better."

"You are very brave."

"Why? Because some guy is going to hypnotize me?"

"Because only a warrior would go back to that night."

"Thanks," I said quietly.

I hung up the phone and thought about it. I would go back to that night if it meant catching her killer. In truth, I'd been going back to that night again and again for twenty years.

Chapter 20

I was lying on a comfortable leather couch, my head resting on the arm. The lights were dim. A Lucite clock rested on the bookshelves in front of me, and I focused for the moment on its tick, tick, tock.

Ben Sato was out of my line of sight. Lewis was in the waiting room with Tommy Salami, because I decided it was more likely I'd laugh or make a wisecrack with Lewis there than let go. Really let go. And fall backward into time.

The psychologist's name was George Guinness. He reminded me of the original father of psychology himself, Sigmund Freud, with a trimmed, clipped grayish beard. Or maybe Santa Claus was a better description, for though George wasn't fat, he was jovial, with reddish cheeks. He was a stereotype right down to his tweed sport coat, and I could smell ever so subtly the faint scent of pipe tobacco.

Ben and I had explained to him what happened to my mother, and how we were hoping we could maybe unearth something I'd repressed in my subconscious mind, forgotten or pushed away as too painful.

After my mother was murdered, I had told police with certainty that a man had been in the house—a man I never actually saw. My mother had called out to him that she would be just a moment. She had seemed unnerved. But with suspicion falling on my father, and Mikey asleep at the time and unable to recall anything, the police considered my story the unreliable testimony of a little girl who didn't want to believe her mother could have abandoned her children.

Before I even got there Ben had met with

George to map out some of the questions to ask. If Ben was anything like me, he was just as anxious to see what, if anything, my little-girl brain could recall.

George Guinness started by asking me to shut my eyes. I tried not to feel self-conscious. He turned on a faint white-noise machine to block out any sounds but his voice. Ben reached out his hand and patted my shoulder, then I could hear him lean back against his leather chair, and I concentrated on George's voice.

Unlike movies or television, the process of hypnosis isn't instantaneous. No one holds up a pocket watch for you to look at going back and forth, back and forth. In fact, the person being hypnotized does a lot of the work. George instructed me to breathe deeply, concentrating on my breath, in and out, belly breathing like in yoga. With each breath, I was supposed to relax into the couch, my body becoming heavy. Then he had me relax each muscle group in isolation.

At all times his voice was calming, soothing, monotone yet not negative. "Tighten all the muscles in your left calf. Tighten, tighten, as I count to five. One, two, three, four, five. Now release. Release and relax. Your leg feels heavier as it sinks into the couch in a pleasant state of deep relaxation. With each breath you are going deeper, deeper, deeper into relaxation.

"Excellent. Now you will tighten the muscles of your left thigh. Breathe deeper as I count to five. Tighten, one, two, three, four, five…"

At some point, I drifted off. It felt like sleep— and yet not. And George told me in this place, this relaxed state, I would answer his questions.

I could hear him, as if he were far off down a tunnel. In the distance. I heard him and I heard myself. My voice was foreign, not my own. It was breathy, sleepy, quiet, as if I might doze off at any moment. Relaxed. Peaceful. George reminded me I was safe. He was there. Ben was there. Nothing bad could happen to me. Nothing could harm me.

First George had me describe the house. My room. My doll. I could see details as if the colors were fresher. I was *there.*

My mother came into the room. I smelled her perfume. I was aware of myself talking to George, but the words fell from my mouth uncensored, without thinking, as if releasing gentle butterflies that fluttered away. I was conscious of them but they flitted around me, and I forgot them as soon as I spoke them. I didn't worry, because George told me not to. And because I knew he was taping me.

She leaned down to kiss me, stroking my hair, my face. I saw a tear in her eye. Her voice quivering ever so slightly.

Then I came to the part when my mother said she had to leave. I tossed my head from side to side. So George said he was going to take me still deeper into my trance.

And then the world went black.

I heard my voice—what I knew to be my voice, only I wouldn't have recognized it— speaking on tape.

"This is creepy," I whispered. Lewis nodded. Ben was staring at the tape recorder on the table as if it were alive. George just kept nodding.

"You were an excellent subject. Went very deep, Billie."

GEORGE: And what is your mother saying to you, Billie?
BILLIE: Don't be afraid, Billie. Mama loves you. Whatever you hear, you stay up

here. Don't come down. No matter what. No matter what, Billie, I don't want you to come out of the room. Oh…she's afraid.

GEORGE: Your mother?

BILLIE: There's a shadow. A man is in the hallway. She's talking to him. *"Just one minute, Andrew. Please."*

GEORGE: Can you see Andrew?

BILLIE: No. I see his shadow. But Mama… she leaves with him. I hear her. *"Don't hurt them and I will go with you."*

I burst into tears, as Lewis handed me a tissue. I couldn't even speak. Lewis stood and walked around the table to my chair and wrapped me in a hug. After a minute or two, I calmed down a bit, though I was trembling.

Ben pressed Stop. "You *did* recall his name. You never did that before?"

I shook my head. "I affected her voice. Did you hear that? I almost sound like her."

"So now what?" Lewis looked at Ben.

"Now we go back to the original interviews again. We go back to every neighbor, every person who could have possibly crossed paths with

Billie's mother. We look for an adolescent boy, or a young man, named Andrew."

I looked resolutely at Lewis, my voice more certain. "We're going to get him."

"Yes." Lewis stared back at me. "But let's do it quickly before he gets you in the bargain."

Chapter 21

I was exhausted. I spent my days at the lab and my evenings with Ben Sato interviewing people exhaustively. We couldn't find any Andrew connected to my mother in any way. Not through her Sunday school class, though we combed through the church registration lists that one *very* organized and anal-retentive church secretary kept as far back as 1972.

We interviewed our neighbors. No one knew an Andrew, remembered an Andrew or was related to an Andrew.

We hunted down people who had moved away.

I tried to talk to my father when we were in Quinn's one night.

"I have a lead, Dad. Into her murder. A name. It's the guy, Dad. The guy who left me the lock of hair. It's him."

We were sitting at a table while around us the typical bar crowd was noisy and laughing. He stood up abruptly. "I can't, Billie." His voice was hoarse.

"But, Dad…"

"Look, I know you want to catch him. And that way you can put her to rest. But I had to put her to rest a long time ago or I would have crawled into that grave with her and left you and your brother orphans. I can't. I can't relive it another second. And I can't stand the thought of this bastard knowing who you are and where you live."

"So help me get him."

"I can't." He lifted the shot glass of bourbon on the table and downed it in one swift gulp. Then he shook his head, wiped at his eyes and went to the back room of Quinn's. The rest of the night he avoided me. But Mikey found me. And my brother was pissed off.

"Look, Billie…you know Dad loves you, right?"

"Of course."

"Have you taken a hard look in the mirror lately?"

"What the hell is that supposed to mean?"

"You look like total shit. How long are you supposed to keep going like this? No sleep. Crappy food. Tommy Salami says some nights you go home at 1:00 a.m. and you're up by 4:45. You're killin' the poor Salami."

"He can stop babysitting me. No one's forcing him to keep the hours I do."

"Come off it, Billie. It's not just the lack of sleep. It's your life."

I looked at my brother. We could pass as twins. Both of us were black Irish—blue eyes, black hair. He had the girls chasing him for as long as I can remember—and for as long as I can remember, he only loved Marybeth, his child-hood sweetheart. He was a one-woman man, no matter how many others threw themselves at him. But as close as Mikey and I were, right about now, I wanted to deck him.

"My life?" I screeched. Some people at the next table looked over their shoulders at us. "My life?" I said in as loud a whisper as I could muster.

"Yes. You're spending all your time with that detective. David's worried sick. Lewis is a mess."

"Lewis is a mess because C.C. hasn't come back yet and because Hollywood is dangling so much money he would never be able to spend it all," I countered.

"And what if you can't solve it, Billie? What if all this just gets you killed? You'd do that to Dad and me? I couldn't take it. That would be it. I'd just want to check out."

"It's not like I'm doing this *to* anyone. Least of all you and Dad. I'm doing it *for* you. For us. So we know once and for all what happened that night."

"Billie...I'm glad you do what you do. But your obsession is hurting everyone around you."

"Don't you want him caught?"

"Not if it means this. Not if I lose you, Billie."

"You know, Mikey...you've called me to post bail for you at 3:00 a.m. more times than I can count on one hand. More times than I can count on *two* hands. I have to go to *toes* to count 'em. And I was always there for you."

With that I stood up and walked out of Quinn's. I was emotionally spent and tired and had nothing to show for my weariness but hurt relationships. Even Bo seemed sulky. I needed a break. Luck. A miracle.

Or a piece of DNA.

Chapter 22

Maybe my mother was watching out for me. Maybe, as Lewis often told me, murder victims linger near the living until they get justice.

We had a match.

While we were processing rape kits, we had three matches actually. Two rapes from the last twenty years. One match was made from two tiny drops of semen. But it was enough.

And when the saliva from the envelope was processed, along with the pant leg specimen, my mother's murderer was suddenly a serial rapist, at the very least—because that was the third match.

Lewis looked with amazement at the results. "Is Ben pulling the old case files?"

"Yeah. We have to find the common thread. Find the link, and we find the killer."

"You make it sound so easy."

I looked at him across the desk. "Not easy, but the little spirals of DNA are starting to come back to haunt him. Two more lives to look at. Two more chances to find a slip-up. To figure out who he is. We find an Andrew in either of their lives and we have him, Lewis."

I was elated at this break. Lewis's phone then buzzed. I listened to his half of the conversation. Saw him cock his eyebrow. Nod. Look puzzled. Nod again. Say "Hmmm." Then he said, "Yes, she's here." Now it was really driving me nuts. Finally, he hung up.

"Well?"

"That was Joe. He wants us to meet with him at seven at his house. Ben Sato will be there."

"Ben?" I was puzzled. "What do the Justice

Foundation and Joe have to do with my mother's case?" I wasn't even aware Ben knew Joe.

"That, Wilhelmina, I have no idea. But like you, I'm dyin' to find out."

At seven o'clock, having sent Tommy Salami home, Lewis and I arrived at Joe's mansion in Alpine, New Jersey. It had a long, sweeping driveway, and Japanese lanterns illuminated the walkway to the ten-foot-high double front door, which was carved from wood and inlaid with a dragon. We rang the bell.

And C.C. answered.

My eyes welled, and I immediately looked to my left at Lewis. As God is my witness, he grabbed me I think to keep his knees from buckling.

Sister Catherine Christine was as beautiful as when she left for her retreat months before, with long strawberry-blond hair so curly it looked as if it was set in ringlets, porcelain skin and an elegant bone structure. "Hello, Lewis," she whispered. "Hello, Billie."

Lewis was still holding my arm. In all the time I've known him, he'd never fallen for any woman. I think he purposely kept women at bay—they never would live up to his high ideals and intellect. His morbid sense of humor, garnered through working with death on a regular basis, meant he was frankly an odd choice for a date. But the minute he laid eyes on C.C. he had loved her, pure and simple, yet he had never so much as kissed her.

He understood she was unhappy with her order before she ever met him, but he certainly didn't intend to confuse her or add to her spiritual burden. Their intellectual connection just happened. Maybe he was right. Maybe they were two halves of one whole. Maybe they were Jungian soul mates. If, according to Lewis, Ben was the warrior and I was the intellect to make one whole, then in the other pairing Lewis was the intellect and C.C. was the spiritual and intuitive.

Their eyes were locked on each other, and I felt a palpable connection between them—not so much sexual as of the soul and spirit. I held my breath.

"I'm sorry to surprise you like this, Lewis. I…left my order. Not because of you— entirely. Because my work was never really approved of. Too activist. Giving spiritual counsel to prisoners is one thing, actively seeking their release is another. But I'm here with no expecta—"

She didn't even get the word out. He rushed to her and grabbed her in a fierce embrace that made my stomach dip just witnessing it. He didn't kiss her—not Lewis's style. They had so much to talk about. But I knew it would all be okay.

Finally they released each other and held hands. My face was wet—had I cried just seeing this scene? Lewis's eyes were shining and wet, and C.C. had tears blatantly streaming down her cheeks. I ran to her and hugged her. "We've needed you." I leaned closer to her and whispered in her ear, "Joe, Lewis…we're all falling apart. You're our glue."

She kissed my cheek. "I'm back for good."

Feeling a surge of hope, I followed C.C. and Lewis into Joe's kitchen, which was cavernous and would make a Michelin-starred chef salivate with envy. Ben was waiting with Joe.

"Well, the gang's all here," Joe smiled. "And we have a new case."

Ben opened up a file folder on the table and spread out photos of a particularly brutal crime scene. "One more match turned up."

"A murder?" I asked.

Ben nodded grimly. "And I think an innocent

man is in jail for it. Which is why I came to Joe. I'm looking at all this on my own clock. No one in the force likes a cop who thinks another cop made a big mistake. I don't want to accuse anyone of dishonor. But this looks very bad."

"So map it out for us," C.C. said. I smiled as soon as she spoke. It was so good just having her there, her energy, her friendship. Lewis was stroking her hand.

"Billie's mother was his first, which was Billie's feeling, too." Ben said. "Billie thinks he was an adolescent, judging by his handwriting. Claire Quinn was murdered. Her case wasn't even pursued for some time—you all know the story there. Then we have these two rapes. In both cases, the women were mothers, early thirties, each with a son and daughter almost identical in age to Billie and her brother—and in both cases, looking very much like them—dark-haired, pale eyes. The women were brutalized by a man wearing a mask. But the crimes were years and towns apart. In one case the woman survived because a car pulled into the driveway—it actually was someone turning around—lost. A simple stroke of fate saved her life."

"And the other?"

"She was raped while her children slept. But she had a restraining order out on an ex-boyfriend and the cops thought that's who it was. The relationship was volatile—reconciling, breaking up, reconciling again. So when she said she was positive it wasn't her boyfriend, I'm thinking they didn't believe her."

"Why do you think she wasn't killed?"

"Apparently, our serial killer was staging things. He took a lock of her hair. He made her dress in a nightgown. He put a set of pearls on her. The little boy woke up, walking into the bedroom all sleepy, wanting to stay in Mommy's bed because of a nightmare, and the rapist freaked out. I think our killer is reenacting a traumatic event. And the boy is *him*."

"So when the little boy got upset," C.C. posited, "he couldn't go through with it."

"Exactly. Which leads us to this murder. It happened four years ago down in Wayne. Mother killed while her two kids are home—boy and a girl, black hair, blue eyes. Dad was home but says he was hit on the head while he was sleeping. Has a major welt to show for it. He says he blacked out. When he woke up his wife was dead."

"Wait," Lewis said. "The Colton murder. It was all over the papers."

I remembered, now, too. The father was a surgeon, and the chilliest bastard you ever saw on the witness stand. Even though other scant evidence existed—a drop of semen, a lone pubic hair not belonging to the victim or her husband— his wildly improbable story, coupled with the fact that he was having an affair, that *she* was having an affair—though her lover had an airtight alibi— and that the doctor was smug, condescending and showed not an ounce of grief on the stand convicted him. He proclaimed his innocence, but he was convicted on personality, not science. Wouldn't be the first time. After all, OJ walked with plenty of science to back up a conviction. Happens all the time.

Ben said, "In rapes, in serial murders, you are usually, in terms of profiling, looking for a connection between the women. Maybe they're all blond or brunette, or have some similar physicality. But when I saw these children in these cases, and I thought of the Colton kids, I looked at the match for what was left at the crime scene with these new matches and we had one."

"So now we go and interview Dr. Colton in jail…see if our C.C. lie detector picks up anything," said Joe. "And we look for a common link in the kids."

Ben nodded, but looked puzzled. "C.C. lie detector?"

Joe beamed at his partner. "C.C. here is better than anything you detectives could possibly rig up as far as telling who's a liar…or who's guilty or innocent. Her instincts are perfect."

"That and a little divine guidance," she said. She had always considered her prison ministry to be like tending modernday lepers. This beautiful woman walked fearlessly into prisons to face down men convicted of the most heinous crimes imaginable. She would, she told me once, murmur the Twenty-Third Psalm as she walked.

"The Lord is my shepherd. I shall not want."

God was always her shepherd. And God also seemed to give her some sort of divination. Every prisoner she met said he was innocent. So we had to choose our cases based on some intuitive faith in the person's story. C.C. was our intuition. She was our faith. She was the staff of Moses. Then we had to hope that DNA could clear them. That science would provide the evidence we needed.

"Well, we have our work cut out for us, don't we?" C.C. said. "Now, instead of one case, we've got four."

I nodded. I stared down at the folders. The little girls *did* look remarkably like me, the boys like Mikey.

"Wait a minute!"

"What?" Lewis asked me.

"If Ben is right in his hypothesis that he's re-enacting a crime, then there's an original crime. Look…" I spread out photos. "Get me pictures of the kids."

We lined them all up, including, eerily, snapshots of Mikey and me in our pj's the night of my mother's murder.

"Look. All these kids have black hair, blue eyes. Same ages. Now, what if our killer witnessed his mother being murdered when he was little, and for some reason, over and over again he's reenacting the crime. The little boy is him. The little girl his sister. The victims are the mother. But why? Why reenact a horrible crime in his own family?"

"To control the outcome," Lewis said. "Ben stated one of the women thought he was staging the scene. He is working through something… But why kill the mother? You'd think he'd want to save her."

Ben stared down, concentrating. "Billie, if he was an adolescent when he killed your mother, let's place his age at eighteen. Strong enough to be able to harm her. Young enough that he was still new at it. How old was Mikey?"

"Nine."

"So let's look at similar crimes ten years *before* your mother's murder."

"But these murders aren't concentrated in one town."

"I'll make some calls," Ben said.

"Oh, and C.C.?" I said.

"Hmm?"

"When you interview Dr. Colton, drop the name Andrew and see what his reaction is."

"Okay. The Justice Foundation is back in full swing," she said.

I grinned to myself. Mikey liked to call us the

Scooby-do Gang. Either way, the power of four—and with Ben, now five—was greater than our power as individuals. If we could keep the foundation from falling apart, we could finally let my mother rest in peace.

Chapter 23

C.C. called me the next afternoon around five o'clock. She was with Lewis at the prison where Dr. Colton was being held.

"The apple doesn't fall far from the tree."

"What do you mean?" I was in the lab sifting through more evidence from the cases. Lewis had taken the day off to spend it with C.C. and to go to meet Dr. Colton with her. Mostly, I assumed, they had a lot of things to say to each other.

I stopped what I was doing and sat down at my

computer. I clicked onto my Internet connection and pulled down a bookmarked page I had found of Dr. Colton. He was handsome in that country-club perfect kind of way—like a Brooks Brothers model. I wondered what prison was like for him. From surgeon to disgrace.

"He's a sociopath, Billie."

"He did it?" Even in the pictures, the surgeon's eyes were cold and flat, emotionless. He was a man who lost his wife and never shed a public tear. But it was beyond stoicism. He just seemed to feel nothing, as if her death was an inconvenience on his schedule.

"I didn't say that."

"So what are you saying?"

Her connection broke up a bit.

"Where are you?" I asked.

"Lewis and I are driving to Nyack. We're on 9W. Mountain must be blocking my signal." She cut out again, but came back. "I'll explain about the doctor. But first, listen to me, the killer's name is Andrew Colton, the good doctor's son."

"His son? But that little boy wasn't even born when my mother was killed."

"No, he wasn't. But his older half brother, Andrew, was."

I felt a chill pass over me. "What?" I asked hoarsely.

"Dr. Colton is a sociopath, Billie. A very smart one with sadist tendencies. In the trial, one thing that came out was his poor relationship with his wife, the way he would humiliate her. One thing that helped convict him were the magazines he subscribed to. Major S&M and fetish publications. He is very, very controlling. He was literally seething just from my asking him questions. No wonder he was convicted—the jury probably despised him. But he didn't do it."

"How do you know?"

"Billie, that man is so arrogant, he would take credit for creating the universe if he thought I'd believe it. Major God complex. I think if he did it, he'd take credit for it. And he would have done it better."

"Better? C.C., isn't taking a life in and of itself a God complex?"

"Yes, but it wouldn't be so sloppy. He would have controlled more."

"Was the first marriage brought up at trial?"

"No. He left that marriage when the boy was eight, and his ex-wife is deceased. It wasn't raised."

"How did she die?"

"According to Colton, she was a suicide."

"You think that's true?"

"I have no idea. But we're doing all this on the fly. Ben has pulled some other detectives in on this. Billie, honey, he is in so much trouble. His lieutenant is furious he's been doing all this side work. But at least with more manpower right now, we can get information faster."

"So Andrew is working through his hatred of the father?" My head was swimming.

"I think so. And think about it. When he killed his father's new wife, framing his father, destroying that family, it was the ultimate, total revenge."

"But the doctor never suspected his son?"

"Not until I brought up the name. Then you should have seen the rage. This guy is capable of murder. I almost feel it's frightening that we're going to clear him…that's how utterly devoid of humanity he is."

"Does he have any idea where his son is?"

"None."

"Wait a minute, there has to be a sister. Where is she?"

"Her name is Mallory Colton. She lives in Nyack, New York. We've called her to warn her. And we're on our way. Ben Sato is meeting us at her place in about two hours."

"Be careful, C.C."

"I will."

"Call me the second you learn anything."

"I will."

I hung up the phone and stared at the pictures of the surgeon. He was languishing in prison, framed by his own son. What had the father done to his first family, to his first wife, to arouse such a hatred in his child?

I couldn't believe the rapid changes in my mother's case in a few short hours.

Now I had a name. Hopefully soon we would have a face. And a reason and motive.

Andrew Colton.

I wondered if he knew he had left me genetic clues through the years. Traces of unspeakable crimes. Traces of his DNA. Traces of his guilt.

Chapter 24

I drove home, my cell phone on my lap, waiting to hear from C.C. and Lewis. David had said he was cooking dinner. It was going to be the first meal we'd eaten together in ages, other than shared English muffins at the breakfast counter once in a while.

When I walked in the door, the table was set, candles were lit, and roses were in a vase. Bo came over to me for a pat, and David popped his head out from the bedroom.

"Hello, gorgeous. Bottle of wine on the counter. Pour yourself a glass."

I walked over to the counter, and next to my wineglass was a small box with a bow on top.

"Open it," he called out.

I lifted the lid.

It was a diamond ring.

David came out of the bedroom, and I felt him behind me. I didn't turn as he wrapped his arms around my waist. "I want to marry you, Billie Quinn. I lost ten years of my life, and I don't want to waste even another second without you by my side. Marry me." He spun me around.

"Yes," I breathed.

"I love you," he whispered, and ran his lips along the nape of my neck.

I shivered slightly. "It's beautiful."

"I know you have your mother's ring, too, but I wanted to get you something that reminded me of you."

I was still stunned and now looked at the diamond. It was beautiful and heart shaped.

"You have my heart. You had it from the first time you walked into prison and told me you believed me. I knew right then I wanted to marry you, even though I didn't dare dream of freedom. Of having a life. Of having a woman. I ached for you."

"Stop," I said, as a sob escaped me. A happy sob. "Please...I love you."

"I'm sorry we've been out of synch." He started kissing my tears.

"You could make it up to me," I murmured. I wrapped my arms around his neck and gave him a lingering kiss. He moved his hands down the small of my back and pulled me closer to him. As always I felt a physical connection between us. I think, when we made love, a part of our hearts remembered his imprisonment and isolation, and so we would connect with that much more intensity, as if to erase that, to heal.

He started seductively biting my ear. And then my cell phone rang. Both of us stopped.

"That's got to be C.C. They figured out the identity of my mother's killer. We're getting close." I couldn't believe that the universe was going to operate in such a way that I would agree to marry my lover and solve my mother's case on one fateful night.

"Answer it," he said, handing me the phone.

"Let's hope they got this son of a bitch. Then we'll have double reason to celebrate."

When I looked at the Caller ID, it said it was my father calling. Before I could answer, it clicked over to my voice mail.

"It's my Dad," I said to David, weighing whether to retrieve the message now or not. I figured he was calling to make up with me. Or to try to convince me to call Mikey—my brother and I were on the outs since that night at Quinns. It was the first time since we were teenagers that we were not communicating.

Sighing, I knew it would bother me if I didn't find out what message Dad had left, but I also knew if he was negative it was going to kill my mood with David. On the other hand, I did have happy news to share. I could just imagine the blow-out party at Quinn's Pub, and I found myself grinning deliriously.

"You know you won't be able to enjoy dinner. You might as well call him. And by the way? That smell is a very nice pan-seared tuna steak with lime sauce. Call him." He kissed me and brushed a stray hair from my face.

David liked to experiment in the kitchen after

ten years of prison food—potatoes from a box and unidentified goulash. Right after his release, he'd gained twenty pounds just enjoying all the things he'd missed.

"All right," I said. "But then dinner and—" I leaned in and kissed his neck "—dessert."

"You got it, the future Mrs. Falco." He turned and went over to the stove to check on his creation. I saw him peering into simmering pots and pans. I was never one to cook, so I smiled at the sight of him tending to our romantic meal. I dialed my voice mail.

"Hello, Billie? It's Daddy. Listen…you won't believe this, but I've got a guy coming over in about a half hour to buy the house. I was working in the yard and he drove by, said he was interested in the neighborhood, did I know any homes for sale. I mentioned I was thinking about it. Anyway, he's coming here tonight. Serious about making an offer. Said he's bringing his checkbook. I know you would rather have had me talk about this more with you. Listen…I love you. I love your brother. Let's get together at Quinn's on Sunday."

I frowned as I pressed the button for delete.

"What's up?" David asked.

"Someone's making my father an offer on the house tonight. I'm just sad."

"When did he put it on the market?"

"He hasn't. Someone just driving by."

"That's weird."

"It happens, I suppose." Then I looked at David. "You know, someone was in my old treehouse that night. You don't suppose…"

"Call your dad." David's voice was intense.

My heart was pounding. Because I had been at the house essentially snooping for my own father's DNA, I never told him about the man in the treehouse. My father was vulnerable, and it was my fault.

I dialed my father's number and someone else answered.

"Hello, Billie."

"Who's this?"

"Daddy."

I gripped the countertop. "Put my father on."

"I don't think so. Your father is a little…indisposed at the moment. Come to the house. Alone. I see a cop, your father's dead before any of you even reach the front door. Remember. Alone. Just you and me, beautiful."

The line went dead.

"He has my father."

"Call 911."

"If he sees police, he'll kill him. Come on."

I ran to my hall closet and pulled out my handgun. David turned off the stove, and almost as if of one mind, we left the apartment with barely a word between us and ran down the street to my car.

"You drive," I told him. "I'm going to make phone calls."

He nodded, and our tires squealed as we pulled away from the curb. I gave David directions the fastest way to Dad's, and then called Lewis's cell phone. I rocked back against the seat slightly, trying to comfort myself and calm down.

"Lewis? I found him. He's got my father. At Dad's house. But I can't call 911 because he says if he sees cops it's all over. I'm on my way over there."

"Billie," his voice was hoarse. "Don't."

"I have to. I heard his voice, Lewis. He's going to hurt my father."

"I've seen his handiwork, sweetie. Don't." I heard a thickening in his voice.

"So have I, but I can't just send squad cars

over there, sirens blazing. This guy is smart, Lewis." I pointed at the exit sign above the highway to David.

"No, Billie…I mean, C.C. and I are here at his sister's home and she's dead. I have *seen* his handiwork."

"Oh, my God. Call Ben."

"Already have. He's on his way here. Maybe fifteen minutes away."

"Well, call him again and send him to my Dad's. With SWAT." I had no choice. I prayed the cops would be careful, hidden.

I hung up the phone. "Can you drive any faster, David?" I looked at the speedometer. He was already doing a solid eighty-five miles per hour.

He pressed his foot almost to the floor. I muttered a nearly silent Hail Mary—all those years of catechism coming back to me.

"Lewis said he murdered his own sister."

"Shit."

Our tires squealed, and it seemed like we were sliding across the road.

"Hang on, Billie," he said, grappling with the wheel. I slid in my seat, despite the seat belt I wore.

We careened across the road, and I started

talking fast to get us of like mind when we reached Dad's house. "We'll both go in, but you stay behind me a little. I have my gun, you take the tire iron from the trunk. Hopefully, as long as he doesn't hear sirens, he won't panic. If he's got my Dad, we just keep him talking. Eventually Lewis and Ben will arrive."

"I don't like this."

"Neither do I. But I feel like I've been waiting for this showdown since that night. If he wants a face-off with me, he's got one. But he's not going to kill my dad."

Brakes screeching, we pulled into Dad's driveway about ten minutes later. No lights were on in the house. We got out. It was a classic summer evening, with thousands of chirping crickets and fireflies glowing as they did their dance across the yard. For a second I thought of Mikey and me, laughing hysterically as we chased the glowing bugs, capturing them and putting them in the empty mayonnaise jar my father had, holes punctured in the lid. My mom would point out the bugs— "There's one. He's glowing biggest of all." Summer nights of laziness and joy. All that had been shattered by Andrew.

I opened the trunk, got the tire iron for David. "Show no mercy," I told him. "He's a serial killer."

David nodded. Then he put the tire iron down for a second on the trunk, and he took both his hands and wrapped one on each side of my face. He kissed me fiercely. "Know, Billie, know I love you with every molecule in my body."

"Me, too. Let's do this."

With a nod, he grabbed the tire iron again, and following behind me, ducking by bushes for cover, we raced up the steps and into the house. I had my gun drawn.

"Dad? Andrew? Dad!" I called out into the darkness. My voice just echoed slightly, bouncing in the silence.

"On three," I said to David. "One, two, three…" I flicked on the first lights in the house. There had been a struggle in the living room. But no blood, thank God. No sign of Dad, either, though.

Room by room we wandered through the downstairs. When we got to the den, the television was on.

"Jesus Christ," I whispered.

"What?" David asked.

"The TV."

The newscaster looked straight ahead at the screen, and David and I were illuminated in the bluish tint of the television light.

"An Amber Alert has been issued in New York and New Jersey for a twin brother and sister. Annie and Josh Barton, who were snatched in broad daylight from their nanny, who was stabbed during the incident."

The screen went to a montage of images of an ambulance, a woman being wheeled into a hospital on a stretcher, and a house shown with police tape all around it.

"The nanny, Carla Chisolm, is in satisfactory condition at Nyack Hospital, and the kidnapper was seen speeding south on route 9W in a white van."

The montage changed to two little faces frozen on the screen, a boy and a girl.

Now the anchor's voice spoke over the pictures, "The first three letters of the license plate are IKL Anyone who has any information…"

"Look at them," I said to David. I was absolutely frozen in place.

The little boy and his sister could have been Mikey and me on the night my mother was taken from us.

"They look just like you."

"I know."

Whatever was going on in the mind of Andrew Colton, he was playing out his fantasies tonight. And he wanted me to be part of them.

Chapter 25

I turned off the television, just not wanting to hear any more. Had he left the TV on to unnerve me? Or, worse, had Dad been watching television, innocently unaware he was being stalked. In my mind I pictured an act of violence occurring right here, my father being murdered. I shook my head to chase the image from my brain.

"Let's check upstairs."

David nodded, and we crept to the staircase.

"Let me go up first," he whispered.

"I have the gun."

"Look…just let me go first. If he gets me, you can shoot him." David cut me off at the stairwell and started up ahead of me. My heart pounded so loudly in my own ears, I felt like David could hear it. Swallowing hard, I tried to calm myself, but it wasn't working.

We went to my old bedroom. Nothing seemed amiss. Dad had never taken down my floral pink wallpaper, and on the shelves sat dolls and the usual artifacts of a teenage girl, yearbooks and photos and souvenirs of proms and vacations. I walked to the closet.

"On three," I whispered, and opened it just like I had seen cops do on television shows forever. "One, two, three," I opened it and aimed my gun into the blackness of the closet.

Nothing. My closet was full of my father's off-season clothes and a couple of boxes of my old stuffed animals, labeled. I don't know why we had never thrown them out. Guess I didn't have the heart to toss my old teddy bears and stuffed dogs and carnival prizes into the trash.

David and I moved along to Mikey's old room, which Dad now used mainly to store junk. Dad's unused exercise bike was gathering dust. A treadmill stood in one corner. This, my father called his "gym." I smiled to myself. Yeah. I'm sure Dad hadn't been in that room in a year.

In the master bedroom, everything was neat as a pin, except Andrew had taken a picture of me from a frame, and placed it on the pillow next to another souvenir—a long lock of black hair.

"What, does he scalp people?" David asked.

"I don't know." I moved closer to the bed. "The blood on this hair is fresh. This is from his sister."

I felt frantic. Where was my father?

"Shit, David. We don't have time to wait for the police. We've got to find him."

I tried to think. I looked out into the yard.

"Let's go to the treehouse," I said, going over to the window. I wondered if he was watching us. Watching and waiting.

David and I ran downstairs and out into the yard. My cell phone rang. I looked at it to see if it was my father's cell phone dialing, but it was Lewis.

"Billie, Ben says to stay away from your dad's place. He's on his way. SWAT is coming."

"Too late, we're here and Dad's not."

"Billie, I'm telling you to get out. Go wait out

front of the house for the police to arrive. Please. Honey, I've never been so worried about a human being my whole life."

"I just have one more place to check, Lewis."

I snapped my phone closed before I could hear him rebuke me. David was three or four steps ahead of me. "David! I'll check the treehouse, you go check the perimeter of the woods, but don't go too far in. If we don't spot him, we'll wait. Ben Sato is coming with the cops." I hoped, at this point, for vans of SWAT teams and helicopters.

David veered over to the left to go searching. I knew Andrew said to come alone, but the situation was out of control. We didn't have flashlights, and there wasn't much of a moon. I scrambled to the treehouse and started climbing up it. Mikey and I had hammered in short pieces of two-by-fours to make steps for a ladder, and then a hole in the floor of the treehouse had a trapdoor over it. Our uncle Tony, the one who owns Quinn's, helped us build it one summer, and we spent nearly every night sleeping in it. We created our own little world that wasn't marred by her murder. We hid from the pain in that treehouse, which is why the thought of my father selling our old house broke my heart.

I pushed on the trap door. Something was partially blocking it. I maneuvered my shoulder and pushed as hard as I could, and whatever it was moved. I positioned my gun and then popped the trap door up. I could see my dad lying on the floor.

"Dad?" I scrambled up into the treehouse. No one else was there. My father was bleeding from a stab wound in his shoulder area. I rushed to his side and put down my gun, and instead pushed on the wound to try to stop the blood flow.

I leaned my head out of the treehouse. "David!" I screamed into the night. "I need help!" I squinted toward the woods, but couldn't see him.

I sat on the floor by my dad. I knew this would all be over soon. I just prayed Ben would get here fast.

I thought of C.C. telling me no matter how long it had been since Lewis and I last talked to God that he was there for us, waiting with open arms.

Dear God…please, please, please let my daddy be okay. Protect us all. Take me. Take me, not him.

I heard David climbing up the treehouse ladder, and his head appeared in trapdoor hole. Then I realized it wasn't David. Or Ben.

I was face-to-face with Andrew Colton.

My mother's killer.

And he looked absolutely, sickeningly delighted to see me.

Chapter 26

I kicked him in the face, and he grunted. I kicked again, then tried to shut the trap door and slam his hands in it. But he was strong. Really strong.

He shoved upward on the trap door, and soon his shoulder and head and arms were in the treehouse, with just his waist and legs down.

"Is that any way to say hello, Billie?"

I dove for my gun, but so did he. Using his palm, he spun the gun away from me to the corner of the treehouse.

I felt trapped. I *was* trapped. I couldn't figure out how I was going to protect my father and fight off Andrew. I knew if I stood, I'd have a height advantage, at least until he got all the way up on the platform.

I got up on my feet, but then realized that was a mistake. I was the adult Billie, not the child Billie—the ceiling of the treehouse was too low to let me stand upright. The treehouse made me have to duck my head. I felt off-kilter, which I guessed was maybe his idea in the first place, a claustrophobic, off-kilter sense of suffocation up there in the darkness. I tried to deliver a roundhouse kick to his neck, but he was quick and grabbed my foot, causing me to fall to the floor on my ass, hard. He twisted my leg, and I was on my side. Old leaves and dampness pressed against my face. I tried to kick my leg free.

Andrew, meanwhile, finished climbing in. I started crawling toward the gun, but he delivered a solid kick to my stomach. I vomited, more like a dry heave, and then sucked for air. Using his foot, he half kicked, half pushed me until my head was down dangling from the square opening in the floor of the treehouse. One more hard shove and I was going face first down the oak tree.

I frantically clawed and used my arms to try to keep from being pushed. Eventually, I was able to maneuver myself so that my legs and butt dangled down, but my arms and head were inside the treehouse. Better to fall feet-first instead of straight down onto my head.

Then he got closer to me. I spat at him and he punched my face, causing me to let go, and I fell to the ground with a heavy thud. Pain radiated throughout my body. I looked down at my leg. It wasn't broken, I didn't think. Or maybe it was. I felt dizzy and rolled onto my side, straining my ears for sirens.

"David!" I screamed. I found I couldn't get onto my hands and knees. My leg *was* broken. It had to be because it wasn't listening to what my brain was trying to tell it. "David!" I shrieked louder. I was frantic. Where was he?

"David!"

I was aware that Andrew was calmly climbing down the ladder. "David can't hear you." Andrew stood over me. "He's dead."

"No!" I heard myself screaming from some-

place very dark and very terrifying. I saw
Andrew's hand coming down to my face. He had
a cloth, which he pressed over my nose and
mouth. And then…only blackness.

Chapter 27

I had no idea how long I was out. None. It could have been an hour. It could have been a week.

When I started to wake up, my head hurt. My leg hurt more. Pain just seared through me and made me almost want to go back to unconsciousness, but I fought to wake up.

My mouth was cottony. It had been that kind of dead unconsciousness where you don't wake refreshed but instead with a panicked, fighting feeling, struggling to clear your mind.

I was in a dark room. Windowless. Maybe a basement. I tried to think back, and only flashes came to me.

Dad lying there bleeding.

The fight with Andrew.

My broken leg.

David.

I bit the inside of my cheek to keep from screaming, but a sob desperately wanted to escape from my chest.

We should have stayed together. I was so desperate to find my father that I may have caused the death of both of them.

I tried to let my eyes adjust to the darkness. I was lying on a queen-size bed, and my hands were duct-taped together. I struggled a bit. There was a little give there. I moved my head and saw stars—I guessed I maybe had a concussion from the fall from the treehouse. Swallowing hard to keep from throwing up, I moved more carefully, more gingerly.

There was nothing I could see that might help me cut the tape. The room had a dresser but no mirror. The bed didn't have a headboard. Nothing else was in the room.

My heart pounded. Panic was the enemy at this point. I had to stay clear-headed. I was desperate for a glass of water.

Above me, I heard someone walking upstairs. I *was* in a basement of some sort. I heard footsteps on a staircase. I tried to steel myself for whatever was coming next.

The door swung open and Andrew stood, illuminated by a bare bulb hanging from a socket in the ceiling.

"Sleep well, my lovely?"

"You didn't have to kill David. You didn't have to hurt my father."

"Sweetheart," he shushed me. "No lovers' quarrels. Please, the children will hear us. I merely eliminated the obstacles to our happiness. In time, you'll see I did the right thing."

This guy was stark, raving mad. But at the mention of the children—the ones from the Amber Alert, no doubt—I knew whatever terror I felt, I needed to keep subdued for their sake. I prayed they were still alive and not dead and posed in some sort of fantasy.

"Where are we?"

"Tsk, tsk, darling. I can't tell you that."

I tried to reason that if he dragged me to the van, with Ben and the police on their way, he couldn't have driven far. They had a partial plate on, the news and people would be on the lookout. He had to have a place to stash us close. I prayed the police were canvasing the neighborhood— whatever neighborhood that was.

Because the media released the partial plate, he would have had to stash the van. Maybe he parked it in a garage and took us into a house. If the police were canvasing, they were surely looking in garages. Please, I thought to myself, please be looking. Don't give up.

Lewis. Ben. C.C. Joe. There was no way they would let me die here. Ben was the best intuitive cop alive. Tommy Two Trees had told Lewis that. With Lewis's scientific mind, C.C.'s spiritual mind and Ben's warrior nature, I prayed they would find me. Me and the children.

I was dying of thirst, and now I noticed he had a glass of water in his left hand. At least it looked like water.

"Thirsty?" He grinned at me.

I was desperately thirsty. I was so thirsty, I couldn't recall ever feeling this way before, not even on the hottest summer day. But I didn't trust him. He could be poisoning me.

"No."

He took a big swig of water from the glass.

"There. I'm not going to kill you this way. Not after I went to all this trouble to get you, darling."

He held the glass to my lips. "Sip."

Despite my utter revulsion at sharing a glass with the man who killed my mother and lover, my fiancé, I sipped. I couldn't fight him if I was dehydrated, if I didn't have a clear mind.

He took his hand and stroked my face. I wanted to bite his hand. He put the glass down and went over to the dresser. He returned with a pair of scissors.

Shit, I thought. Taking my hair, he cut off a lock.

"For my scrapbook," he told me.

Then he stood, and taking the scissors with him, and the lock of hair, he left the room.

I desperately, with a primal fear, wanted to call out to him, to beg for my life. But I also knew that's what he wanted. To play God. And I wasn't going to let him.

A part of me even wondered if I did want to live. *David.*

In the darkness and dampness of the basement room, all I could feel was grief.

I was Achlys.

Grief was my prison.

And then, despite my fear, the drugs betrayed me, and I fell back to sleep.

When I woke again, I was more clear-headed. I guessed more of the drugs had worn off. I felt two things: a crushing sense of grief and intense pain.

Lifting my head, I tried to glimpse my leg. I was wearing jeans. My legs weren't tied, but if I moved my leg at all, I felt excruciating pain tear up and down my nerves from my foot to my hip.

I lay there. Lewis's prophetic words came back to haunt me. Cat and mouse. And now I was in the mousetrap.

Think, Billie, I told myself. Overpowering him would be impossible. I had seen what he was capable of when he scaled the Little League fence and when he fought me in the treehouse.

There was no time to think, though, because Andrew came into the room. This time he turned on a light and a dim bulb in the ceiling came on. I was able to see my bed was a Salvation Army-type cast-off, stained and disgusting. I saw dark-brown stains that looked like old blood. I knew if we tested it, there would be a wealth of evidence there. I consoled myself that when Ben and Lewis found me, even if I was dead, they could nail this bastard. I wanted a needle in his arm.

"Billie, if you're a good girl, and you don't try to run away, I have some dinner waiting for you. The children want to see their mommy. I promised them a new mommy, you know."

I felt queasy with the thought of how much terror these children had to be feeling. It was then I made myself a promise. I would do whatever it took to stay alive. No matter how much pain, no matter how much grief, these children were going to get out of here alive if I had a breath of life in me myself.

"I'll be good," I said, thinking that I wouldn't be able to run away anyway on my broken leg. I was blinking rapidly to get used to the light, which shone rather directly into my eyes, and now I could see Andrew clearly.

He looked just like Mikey. He had black hair and blue eyes, pale skin. He was dressed very nicely, actually, in dark pants and a black T-shirt. His hair was cut neatly. He didn't look anything like a dangerous man. Like a killer. He was like Ted Bundy, like the serial killers that walk amongst us, undetected.

There was one big difference, though, compared to Mikey. My brother's eyes danced. It was what drove women wild. He always looked like he knew a secret inside joke, as if at any moment he was going to burst into laughter. He had charisma. Charm. But Andrew's eyes were as flat and glasslike as a doll's.

They were the eyes of a man without a soul.

"I'm so pleased to hear you'll be good, Billie. I have clothes for you to change into. This gown should fit you." He held up a black peignoir set. A nightgown. "And I have a beautiful necklace for you." He held up pearls. "And if you're very good, I will even give you some pain medication for your leg. It's definitely broken. That's going to be tough."

"I'll manage," I said flatly.

"Good. I'll leave you to change." He put the nightgown and the pearls on the bed with a hairbrush and red lipstick. Then he took the same scissors he had used to cut my hair and he cut the duct tape binding my hands. They felt numb, and I tried to rub them to bring the circulation back.

"Make yourself beautiful for Daddy."

With that, he turned and walked away, shutting the door, and by the sound of it, locking it behind him.

I gingerly tried to sit up. My hands felt like they'd been stung by a hive of bees. Moving sent agonizing pain through my hip and leg. I pulled off my shirt and ever so slowly undid my jeans. Lying back down, I slid out of them as best I could, pulling them down to my thighs, then sitting up again and sliding them down to the floor.

Now I got a look at my leg. It made me feel sick to my stomach. It was mottled and red, and I assumed I was in danger of phlebitis or a blood clot.

I had no time to worry about my leg. I needed to think, think, think. My brain had always been my weapon. I needed to use it.

Pulling the nightgown on over my head, I found it fit me perfectly. I lifted the pearls. They looked like my mother's. Two simple strands. I put them around my neck and then pulled a brush through my hair. My head hurt, so I did it as gently as possible, not tugging.

I lifted the lipstick and looked at the bottom of the tube. It was an old-fashioned-looking case. I squinted to read the shade. This had to be from twenty years ago. I uncapped it and smelled it. The scent was heavy, perfumed, waxy. I touched the lipstick. The texture was nothing like lipsticks available now.

Andrew was having me apply lipstick belonging to his dead mother.

So, feeling as if I was already a certain corpse, I pressed the lipstick to my lips and prayed in my mind for Ben to feel me, his Jungian other half.

Come find me.

Chapter 28

I waited, dressed up like a woman from another time and place, for Andrew Colton to come back. He did, and he had an old woman's cane.

"Here. See if you can walk. I don't have a wheelchair."

He handed me the cane, but he didn't release it.

"And if you try anything, I will slit the children's throats."

"I won't, Andrew," I said, trying to keep the quaver from my voice.

"Good girl."

I took the cane and tried to stand. I saw stars and gasped for breath.

"You shouldn't have fought me in the treehouse."

I wasn't going to comment on what *he* shouldn't have been doing.

I put my foot to the ground. I realized no matter what I did, I was going to be in agony. So, leaning on the cane and biting the inside of my cheek to keep from screaming out, I made my way, an inch at a time, toward the door.

When we got out to the hall, I looked to my right.

"Stairs?" I said incredulously.

"Here." Andrew was beside me. He lifted me in his arms. "I'll carry you up."

We started up the stairs, and I held myself stiffly, not wanting to lean into his body. He smelled of Polo cologne, and close up, he really was very, very handsome. Almost pretty. And yet, I didn't sense I was near a living, breathing human, but next to some sort of psychotic robot.

When we reached the top step, we were in a living room. It was well appointed, with a couch near a window with its blinds drawn and curtains covering them. Two children, the girl in a lacy dress, the boy in dress pants with a perfect crease, a white shirt that was dazzlingly new, and hair slicked back, sat stiffly in chairs.

At the sight of me, the little girl started to cry. The little boy looked dazed. My heart broke for them.

Andrew set me on the couch.

"Now, family, I have dinner cooking. Mommy isn't well, so that's why she's not in the kitchen, but you sit here and tell Mommy about your day."

With that, he left us alone.

"Come here," I whispered at the kids. The little girl rushed to me and buried her face in my chest, grateful I am sure for anyone maternal in this insane situation, terrified.

The little boy just stood and stiffly walked toward me. When he was close up, I could see his pupils were dilated so huge that they were almost blocking out his irises. They had been drugged, too.

Crap. I had never been in such a dire situation in my life. And now I had to think for the three of us. Keep us alive.

In the next room, I could see Andrew ever so slightly if I leaned and peered into the kitchen. I squinted. His back was toward us, and a small black and white television sat on the counter with the sound off. I watched as police were swarming a neighborhood on the screen. The view was from a helicopter.

I leaned back and stroked the girl's hair and then pulled the boy next to me.

Okay. They were going house to house. Andrew knew it. At some point, law of averages, law of numbers, someone was going to knock on this door. If we screamed, Andrew would kill us. If we were silent, would they just assume we weren't home and move on? Had they already while I was lying unconscious?

Think, Billie.

We were playing parts. His mother was a suicide, his father a sadist. He had perhaps witnessed his father controlling the family, abusing the mother, torturing her. That twisted his mind.

Nature versus nurture.

All right. Then what? Had Dr. Colton abandoned his first family and she cracked and then killed herself? Had she, first, turned around and been abusive to her children? Had Andrew been sexually abused? In cases where boys are sexually abused it's sometimes in the guise of him being the "man of the house" with a woman disturbed and husbandless.

I couldn't beat Andrew physically. He was warped though, cracked, mentally tortured. I could beat him with my mind.

I looked at the little girl and boy.

"Listen to me," I whispered to them. "I'm going to try to save us. I need you to act happy. I know you're not happy. You're scared. But we're going to play pretend until the police get here. Okay?"

The boy nodded stiffly. The girl looked at me with a fragment of hope in her eyes.

I knew what I had to do. I had to rewrite Andrew's history. I had to rewrite the history of his parents' marriage. I had to make him believe I loved him, he loved me, and we were the perfect family.

I had to seduce my mother's killer.

Until I had a chance to kill him myself.

Chapter 29

Andrew came out of the kitchen with a plate of little canapé sandwiches. I instantly "got" it. Andrew's father had run the house like something out of the 1950s. Perfect housewife by day. But at night, his twisted mind turned his household into a sexual war zone. It was a sick dichotomy. Canapés. No one made them anymore.

"Here you go. This is from your recipe, honey."

"Thank you, darling," I murmured.

He set the plate down.

"Go ahead, children. Take one," I urged the kids. "They're delicious. I promise."

I could see them struggling between being famished and tired and being terrified. Hunger won out, and they each stuffed one in their mouth.

"Good. I have a roast beef in the oven. Honey, would you like a Manhattan?"

"That would be lovely. I'd make you a drink, honey, but silly me and this hurt leg of mine."

I wondered how he would react to my role playing. But instead of reacting with mistrust, he looked delighted, as if at last someone understood him.

"No problem. I'll make me one, too." He practically skipped back into the kitchen.

I swallowed. This was working. And as sick as I felt inside, sicker still at the thought of him maybe touching me, I knew I would have to go so far as to sleep with him if need be.

I shut my eyes, a vision of David the last time we made love appearing in my head. I chased it away. I had to stay focused.

He returned with an amber-colored Manhattan—two of them actually. He handed me one and then toasted me. "To the perfect wife. The perfect mother. The perfect children."

I raised my glass. "The perfect man, in every way."

He seemed pleased by that compliment.

"Do you think you can make it to the dinner table?"

"Sure, sweetheart. You may have to help me." I put down my Manhattan.

"Carry that in for your mother," he ordered the little boy.

I stared at the boy, urging him with my eyes. "It's okay, honey."

Thank God, he seemed to jolt out of his stupor a little and he picked up the glass and carried it in to the kitchen. The little girl followed him, and then Andrew came to me, helping me to my feet and handing me my cane.

Now that I was moving around a little and not flat on a hard mattress, the pain was still intense, but I was managing to hide it. I limped and struggled, but made it to the kitchen. The table was set with crystal and fancy china.

"This looks lovely," I said.

"Thank you." He pulled out my chair, and I sat down.

The children sat at my left and right, and he sat down at the other head of the table. I looked down. He had actually given me a knife, though it didn't look very sharp. In the roast beef, though, was a sharp carving blade and large fork.

"Are you doing the honors, dear?" I asked him. "I can't stand."

"Oh, of course."

Also on the table were hot rolls, potatoes, corn, beans and a tossed salad. I reached for plates and bowls and served the kids. He placed slices of meat on their plates, then I cut them with the dull knife I had—I practically was sawing the meat just to get it cut into little pieces.

I sipped my Manhattan, grateful for anything to quench my cotton mouth. I saw he had poured the kids milk.

"Grace?" I asked him.

"Of course." He said a simple blessing, "Thank you for this food and family, Amen."

And then we ate. I pretended to, bringing bits of corn to my lips, while scanning the room with my eyes, trying to figure out what I was going to do.

In the end, the only weapon was the carving knife. And just as I was formulating a plan…the doorbell rang.

Chapter 30

The children exchanged glances. I tried not to reveal any emotion.

"Don't answer it," Andrew warned me.

"Darling, I couldn't even get up."

The children watched us, first Andrew, then me, as if following a tennis volley.

"Stay there."

"Of course."

Now the knocks on the door were becoming louder. "Police! Police!"

I knew it. Even if we didn't answer, by now Ben would be utilizing all the powers of the force. All it would take was a search for Andrew Colton's driver's license, a neighbor to say he lives next door. Anything.

It all happened in the blink of an eye. Andrew bolted from his chair and opened a drawer, pulling out a gun. He approached the little girl, as if he was going to take her hostage.

But with one swift move, ignoring every bolt of pain searing through me like fire, I stood, grabbed the carving knife and plunged it in his stomach, twisting and feeling the sickening spurt of blood on my fingers as my hand slid down the blade and I felt it slice my palm.

"Run to the door," I shrieked to the kids, even pushing at the little girl with my free hand, assuring they wouldn't freeze in terror.

They leaped from their chairs and ran, and I could hear them opening the locks on the front door. I locked eyes with Andrew.

I pushed the knife in more, as I heard the police storming in, and out of the corner of my eye, I saw Andrew being shot, even as he leveled the gun at me.

I felt as if someone had just punched me. I lost

my balance, let go of the knife and collapsed to the floor. From that vantage point, I watched his body being riddled by shots and falling next to me. I looked into his cold eyes, always flat, always dead. Only now, I knew he was truly not only soulless but breathless…. He *was* dead.

Ben Sato appeared over me. I heard him say, "She's shot. Bleeding."

Then he leaned in very close to me and whispered in my ear, his lips touching me. "You got him. You're a warrior."

And that's the last thing I remember of the night I caught my mother's killer.

Chapter 31

When I woke up again, I heard the steady beeping of hospital machinery. My eyelids fluttered. Feeling a bit like Dorothy coming to in the *Wizard of Oz*, I looked around and saw all the people I loved. My father, Mikey, Lewis, C.C., Joe and Ben. Then I felt a rush of tears, because he wasn't there.

David was missing.

My father leaned down and kissed me on my forehead, not once, but a hundred times. "I know, baby. I know." His arm was in a sling, and I glimpsed bandages beneath his shirt.

"You okay, Daddy?"

"Except for seeing you like this. Yeah."

I fought to speak, my voice betraying my sadness, "I'd hoped he had lied to me. That David wasn't really dead."

Dad wiped at his eyes. Mikey turned around so I wouldn't see him cry, but his shoulders shook.

"Can you all leave me alone for a bit?" I asked. My heart felt like it had broken all anew.

One by one they nodded, each coming to my bed and kissing me, except for Ben, who simply bowed.

And there, alone in a hospital bed on crisp white sheets, I wept for the man I loved. I wept until no more tears would come. And only then, only then, did I call a nurse and tell her to send in Lewis.

His face popped around the side of the door.

"Wilhelmina, I'm so sorry." He walked in, carrying a plant, which he put on the windowsill. "I know it doesn't help even a tiny bit, but I had to buy you something. I've never felt so useless my entire life."

"What happened?"

Lewis pulled up a chair. Then he took my

hand and caressed it, pulling it to his face, which was prickly.

"You haven't shaved."

"I haven't left here for twenty-four hours." He kissed my palm, which was bandaged and then kissed my fingertips. "Don't ever scare ol' Lewis like that again."

"I'll try not to," I said. It hurt to talk.

"You were shot in the chest. Missed your heart by a mere three inches. Needed surgery. Lost two pints of blood. We all donated. Maybe you even have a little bit of me pumping through your veins."

"God forbid.... Lewis...how did you find me?"

"Well, C.C. and I got to his sister's. That poor girl was lying in bed looking like she was sound asleep, but he had post-mortem done her body up like a corpse. Powder. Lipstick. And she'd been stabbed about a hundred times. Her throat slit. Anger issues," he tried to be his old self, mocking the dead, but his usual smile was very weak and his eyes were wounded.

"Then you called us, and we knew we were in a world of trouble. Later on, not then, but hours later we found out that after Dr. Colton left his first family, the first missus had turned to prostitution. Drank. Drugs. She wasn't so much a suicide as a passive suicide. Died of hepatitis C and alcoholism. She used to turn tricks in front of the children. After her death, Andrew and his sister went to live with their grandmother—who lived in that house we found you in. Not Colton, but her name was Margaret Farmer. He inherited the house upon her death."

"Farmer?"

"Yes."

"Didn't she live next door to the church? The crazy old lady who used to yell at the neighborhood kids?"

"Well, I wasn't there, but from what I hear, yes. Resented the hell out of that boy and girl coming to live with her."

"He had seen my mother at church every Sunday, then. She never missed Mass."

"And your mother looked like his before Mrs. Colton ruined herself on drink and drugs. Anyway, the father had gotten his new family. His perfect family. So he didn't want to be saddled with the kids. Total rejection. Not only that, apparently he was a sadist, as we guessed.

No telling what he did to that poor first wife before she died. Crushed her spirit."

"So Andrew's been spending his life trying to re-create a perfect family so his father won't leave? So his mother won't die?"

"Near as we can figure it. We'll never totally know. Serial killers warp everything. Like a hall of mirrors."

I inhaled and winced.

"Want to ring for your morphine shot?"

"No. Not until I know what happened to David."

Lewis took my hand and rubbed it against his cheek again.

"Well, when you called, we called Ben who did an about-face. He had to call and get backup, SWAT, everything, but try to do it so it wouldn't sound like the army converging on your dad's place and maybe scaring Andrew into killing you all." I saw him inhale to collect himself.

"But by the time they got there, I was gone."

Lewis nodded. "They didn't miss you by but ten minutes, they figure. Max."

"Dad?"

"He was stabbed, but it wasn't as bad as it looked."

And then the question I dreaded asking. "David?"

Lewis put his hand to his eyes, rubbing them hard. Composing himself, he whispered, "Maybe you should rest."

"No. I have to know, Lewis. Don't baby me."

"Heaven forbid that." He shut his eyes. "Okay then. David didn't suffer. Andrew had put a trip wire in the woods, and when David fell, Andrew slit his throat with a hunting knife. It was over in less than a minute." Lewis opened his eyes and looked at me again. "I'm so sorry."

I swallowed hard and looked out the window. "He asked me to marry him." I looked down at my hand where my engagement ring sparkled.

"I saw that. Beautiful ring. He loved you. God, did that man love you."

"I know. I'll never forget the first time we got to touch each other after prison. God...will I ever feel that way about someone again. Shit, Lewis, it hurts so bad. What happened next?"

"Well, Ben got there. They quickly ascertained you were gone. They got your dad to the hospital, but once they stitched him up, he discharged himself AMA—against medical advice. He was in the search, too. And Mikey. And all the Quinns. Cops finally gave up arguing with them all. Too many of them."

I smiled to myself, despite my broken heart.

"They canvased the neighborhood. Figured you couldn't have gone far. He had a van, but they had shut down the town's perimeter. They just went door to door. Every bush, car, garage, house, window, school building. Andrew Colton didn't ring any bells. But then someone mentioned an Andrew *Farmer.*"

"And then they knew where I was."

"Yes. We peeked in the garage and saw the van. And let me tell you, it was the classic, 'But he seemed so normal.' He had a job."

"Doing what?"

"Sold textbooks to schools. Traveled a lot. When he would meet with teachers about course adoptions or travel near schools, he would spot the sibling pairs. That's how he picked his victims."

"Jesus. How are the kids?"

"Oh, you know. They'll need a lot of therapy. Jesus, I feel like I need therapy except I would pity the shrink who tried to treat me. You saved those kids' lives. Their parents have been here.

Want to talk to you when you're up to it. They want to thank you. As for you, almost a compound fracture. Five pins in that leg."

I looked at my leg in a cast, hoisted up in a trapezelike contraption.

"Yeah. You ain't going to look like a beauty queen in a bathing suit with that leg." He winked at me. "Gunshot, I told you about. And that takes you to about here."

"How long was I in that house?"

"Not long. Five hours."

"Seemed like days."

"I know. It had to have." He shook his head. "Don't know how you survived it, Billie. But it was the drugs made it feel like a really long time."

I nodded. "Thanks, Lewis. For finding me."

"Like I said," he stood up. "Don't do that to me again. I love you, you know. In a…well, you know in what way."

"I love you, too. As my best and dearest friend."

"I told Mitch to shove the television job, by the way."

I grinned.

"Yeah," Lewis said sheepishly. "What do I need more money for when I've got my girl?"

"C.C."

"Well, C.C., I love her. But I mean you. Working side by side."

I teared up. "Can you send my dad and Mikey in?"

"Sure thing."

He left, and Dad and my brother came in.

"He won't ever bother us again," I said. "I'm so sorry for all I put you through."

"Don't, Billie," Mikey said. "And I swear to you, I won't ever get in trouble again. I'm on the straight and narrow from now on."

"Hospital bed promises are forgotten when the person recovers, Mikey."

"Not this time."

I knew he meant it. Now. And I knew his heart was in the right place. The same way I knew it would be just a matter of time before he heard of a good score of DVDs or a backroom poker game with high stakes.

"He proposed to me, you know," I told them quietly. I shut my eyes. I thought I was done crying, but I was realizing I might never be done. Not totally.

"He was a good man," my father said.

"I would have been proud to call him my brother-in-law."

"Thanks, Mikey."

"You need your rest," Dad said.

"I know. I love you."

"I love you, too. I think I'm going to stay in that house after all. I think maybe she would want that."

"Can you send in Ben?"

"Sure."

They each kissed me on the top of my head. When they left, I shut my eyes. The pain was pretty intense. An image of Andrew jumped into my head. I opened my eyes to chase it away, and Ben was standing next to my bed.

I expected him to bow, but instead he came over to me, bent over and placed his lips on my forehead. He pulled away and looked me in the eyes and sat in the chair next to the bed. He slid it closer to my bedside.

He put his hand on top of mine, and I was grateful for my friend's touch.

"I may be a warrior, but I was very frightened for you, Billie."

"It was horrible," I whispered.

"I cannot even imagine." He spoke quietly, which I realized was his way. It felt soothing to me. I looked out the window and saw dusk was settling over the sky.

"He held me at one point, carrying me upstairs," I said. "I felt his chest and stomach pressed against me. All I wanted to do was kill him or react, but instead I had to act as if I cared for him. Every nerve in my being wanted to not do it, Ben. But I had to. I had to save the children."

His eyes looked moist. "You saved them. You did a very brave thing. Something most people could not do."

"Those poor babies."

"Just like you and your brother."

I shook my head. "No, we weren't tormented like that. He left us there alone. He just took her."

"I think maybe…maybe your mother saved you. By going with him quietly that night instead of panicking."

"I think you're right."

Just leave the children and I will go with you.

My mother had died so that Mikey and I would live. A mother's total sacrifice.

"We found files on his laptop. He had his next

two sibling pairs picked out. If you hadn't stopped him, he would have kept on killing."

I swallowed hard, wondering if my voice would betray me. "Yes, but…David…"

He hung his head and patted my hand. "I know."

"I thought, if I did this, I would leave the grieving behind. I wouldn't be like Achlys anymore. I would move forward in life." My diamond ring glittered in the light. I would have moved forward. David and I would have had children, and I would have visited my dad in that house and they would have played in the yard and brought life back to the house again. Now I never would move forward. Not ever.

"I thought so, too. I thought it would bring closure. You have made too many sacrifices."

"Is there such a thing? Does God even care about our sacrifices?"

"Sometimes I think the gods know that warriors can bear more tragedy. We are burdened more because we can carry more burden."

"It hurts, Ben."

"I hurt, too. I hurt for you. I rode in the ambulance with you. I talked to you. In your ear. I told you to live. That you had more things yet to do."

We sat in silence for a while. "Ben?"

"Yes, Billie?"

"Did you feel me in that house? Did you feel me calling you?"

"Asking me to find you?"

"Yes."

He nodded.

"What is that?"

"I don't know. I always thought I was a lone warrior. But I think when you have your other half, the other half of how you think, then maybe…I just knew you weren't dead yet, and we had to search harder and faster."

"Are you in big trouble? With your lieutenant and all?"

He gave me a crooked smile. "I *was*. But then CNN and MSNBC and CBS and ABC…and NBC…they all came. Catching a serial killer is big news. Now he's not so mad."

"Funny how things work that way."

"Yes."

I shut my eyes and tried to rest, but again Andrew's face came to me. My eyes shot open. "I keep seeing him in my mind. I hate it. I see him, and I feel like he's here, making me dress for him. I want to burn that nightgown."

"You must replace his face with something else. Try to picture your mother as an angel instead. With David. Or maybe just picture in your mind a happy time. Every time Andrew comes into your mind, you tell him to leave and replace him with the other thought."

"Okay, I'll try."

"I'll let you rest."

He stood, hesitated and leaned down again and kissed my forehead. Then he said, "Shut your eyes. Gently."

I did. Then I felt Ben kiss each eyelid.

"Rest well, my warrior."

"Ben?" I said, keeping my eyes shut.

"Yes?"

"Thanks for finding me."

He touched my cheek, and I heard him leave.

Andrew's face came to me again. But I decided to replace him. I pictured an actual memory, a summer day. Mikey and I were running through the grass chasing butterflies while my mother tended her garden. She laughed watching us, and we ran over to her with dandelions.

"Make a wish, Mama," I said, holding out my "flower."

She shut her eyes, then blew hard. The white milky blossoms floated away.

"Now your wish will come true."

"What did you wish for?" Mikey asked.

"To live to be a very old woman. That way I can bounce my grandbabies on my knee." She kissed us both. We ran. I felt Mikey's hand in mine. It's always been there, his hand in mine.

Then my happy memory changed and took on a new life of its own. I saw my mother clothed in white, like an angel, beaming. And next to her was David. He looked peaceful. No pain. No suffering. From prison to eternity. He and my mother started soaring up to the sky, soaring until they became one with the sun, and all I was left with were warm sunbeams on my face and white light.

And then I fell asleep. A real sleep. Not drugs or hazy sleep. I fell asleep. But I didn't dream.

Chapter 32

My friends and I gathered at David's gravesite. We had buried him months before, but now the headstone was there.

DAVID FALCO
BELOVED SON AND FRIEND
FREE FOREVER

A dove was carved on the stone representing his free flight to heaven. Freedom. Peace. Serenity. Eternity.

I still walked with a limp, but in truth, we were all in the place of Achlys for right now.

After things settled down, Joe broke up with Vanessa. The Justice Foundation—with the addition of Ben as full-time investigator—is in no danger of closing anytime soon. We have too many cases. Too many men imprisoned. Too many people needing release from their grief and their false dungeons.

We also started a David Falco Scholarship Fund for men released from prison to apply to go back to college or night school. That way David could live on with us, still part of the team.

"Should we say something?" Lewis said at the graveside.

"Let C.C." I replied.

She nodded, and Lewis, Ben, Joe and I bowed our heads. A gentle breeze floated over us as she spoke a prayer about freedom, redemption, hope and faith.

"Amen," we each said in turn. Suddenly a hawk took flight and soared overhead. It was eerie, as if it was David.

"That was lovely, C.C.," I said softly. I watched the hawk fly out of sight.

"Thanks. Come on, Lewis, Joe, let's give Billie some time alone."

Lewis came and put his arm around me. "We'll meet up with you at Quinn's. Have a proper memorial dinner for him."

"Sounds good."

The three of them walked toward their car. I had come with Ben.

"I should leave you."

I shook my head. "Please stay."

We stood there in silence. I liked that Ben never seemed to mind silences. After a few minutes I cleared my throat.

"Ben?"

"Yes, Billie."

"Do you believe in heaven?"

"No. I believe in rebirth."

"So you believe David will come back as something else?"

He nodded. "I like to think that."

"Could he come back as a hawk?"

"He could. He could come back as anything. As a new baby. As a hawk. As a tortoise to live a long life."

I stared at the headstone.

"Will I ever leave this place?"

He knew I meant the metaphorical, not the physical. "The grieving place?"

I nodded.

"When I caught the man who killed my sister, I didn't leave. The universe always changes. The grief just became something else. It's still there though."

I bent over and kissed the headstone.

"Come on, Ben," I said.

He offered me his arm to lean on, and we walked across the grass. Autumn was coming. The leaves were starting to turn red and golden.

I felt a thought come into my mind, like a shadow, of that horrible night. But I lifted my face to the sun. I felt the light. And then, holding on to Ben, I walked away from the grieving place toward a light I didn't yet understand or embrace, but that I knew was there. Waiting for me.

* * * * *

"Oh, no!"

The reaction slipped out before Emma Valentine could stop it, for there stood the very man she most wanted to avoid seeing again.

He didn't look any happier to see her.

"Well, come on, get on board," he said gruffly. "I won't bite." One eyebrow rose. "Though I might nibble a little," he added, mostly to amuse himself.

But she wasn't paying any attention to what he was saying. She was staring at him, taking in the royal blue uniform he was wearing, with gold braid and glistening badges decorating the sleeves, epaulettes and an upright collar. Ribbons and medals covered the breast of the short, fitted jacket. A gold-encrusted sabre hung at his side. And suddenly it was clear to her who this man really was.

She gulped wordlessly. Reaching out, he took her elbow and pulled her aboard. The doors slid closed. And finally she found her tongue.

"You…you're the prince."

He nodded, barely glancing at her. "Yes. Of course."

She raised a hand and covered her mouth for a moment. "I should have known."

"Of course you should have. I don't know why you didn't." He punched the ground-floor button to get the elevator moving again, then turned to look down at her. "A relatively bright five-year-old child would have tumbled to the truth right away."

Her shock faded as her indignation at his tone asserted itself. He might be the prince, but he was still just as annoying as he had been earlier that day.

"A relatively bright five-year-old child without a bump on the head from a badly thrown water polo ball, maybe," she said defensively. She wasn't feeling woozy any longer and she wasn't about to let him bully her, no matter how royal he was. "I was unconscious half the time."

"And just clueless the other half, I guess," he said, looking bemused.

The arrogance of the man was really galling.

"I suppose you think your 'royalness' is so obvious it sort of shimmers around you for all to see?" she challenged. "Or better yet, oozes from your pores like…like sweat on a hot day?"

"Something like that," he acknowledged calmly. "Most people tumble to it pretty quickly. In fact, it's hard to hide even when I want to avoid dealing with it."

"Poor baby," she said, still resenting his manner. "I guess that works better with injured people who are half asleep." Looking at him, she felt a strange emotion she couldn't identify. It was as though she wanted to prove something to him, but she wasn't sure what. "And anyway, you know you did your best to fool me," she added.

His brows knit together as though he really didn't know what she was talking about. "I didn't do a thing."

"You told me your name was Monty."

"It is." He shrugged. "I have a lot of names. Some of them are too rude to be spoken to my face, I'm sure." He glanced at her sideways, his hand on the hilt of his sabre. "Perhaps you're contemplating one of those right now."

You bet I am.

That was what she would like to say. But it suddenly occurred to her that she was supposed to be working for this man. If she wanted to keep the job of coronation chef, maybe she'd better keep her opinions to herself. So she clamped her mouth shut, took a deep breath and looked away, trying hard to calm down.

The elevator ground to a halt and the doors slid open laboriously. She moved to step forward, hoping to make her escape, but his hand shot out again and caught her elbow.

"Wait a minute. *You're* a woman," he said, as though that thought had just presented itself to him.

"That's a rare ability for insight you have there, Your Highness," she snapped before she could stop herself. And then she winced. She was going to have to do better than that if she was going to keep this relationship on an even keel.

But he was ignoring her dig. Nodding, he stared at her with a speculative gleam in his golden eyes. "I've been looking for a woman, but you'll do."

She blanched, stiffening. "I'll do for what?"

He made a head gesture in a direction she knew was opposite of where she was going and his grip tightened on her elbow.

"Come with me," he said abruptly, making it an order.

She dug in her heels, thinking fast. She didn't much like orders. "Wait! I can't. I have to get to the kitchen."

"Not yet. I need you."

"You what?" Her breathless gasp of surprise was soft, but she knew he'd heard it.

"I need you," he said firmly. "Oh, don't look so shocked. I'm not planning to throw you into the hay and have my way with you. I need you for something a bit more mundane than that."

She felt color rushing into her cheeks and she silently begged it to stop. Here she was, formless and stodgy in her chef's whites. No makeup, no stiletto heels. Hardly the picture of the femmes fatales he was undoubtedly used to. The likelihood that he would have any carnal interest in her was remote at best. To have him think she was hysterically defending her virtue was humiliating.

"Well, what if I don't want to go with you?" she said in hopes of deflecting his attention from her blush.

"Too bad."

"What?"

Amusement sparkled in his eyes. He was certainly enjoying this. And that only made her more determined to resist him.

"I'm the prince, remember? And we're in the castle. My orders take precedence. It's that old pesky divine rights thing."

Her jaw jutted out. Despite her embarrassment, she couldn't let that pass.

"Over my free will? Never!"

Exasperation filled his face.

"Hey, call out the historians. Someone will write a book about you and your courageous principles." His eyes glittered sardonically. "But in the meantime, Emma Valentine, you're coming with me."

Silhouette® Desire®

**Introducing an exciting appearance
by legendary
New York Times bestselling author**

DIANA PALMER

HEARTBREAKER

He's the ultimate bachelor...
but he may have just met
the one woman to change his ways!

Join the drama in the story of a confirmed
bachelor, an amnesiac beauty and their
unexpected passionate romance.

---

*"Diana Palmer is a mesmerizing storyteller
who captures the essence of what
a romance should be."—Affaire de Coeur*

**Heartbreaker *is available from Silhouette Desire
in September 2006.***

Silhouette®
BOMBSHELL™

COMING NEXT MONTH

#105 SPIN CONTROL by Kate Donovan

Defending FBI agent Justin Russo against a murder rap would take every skill in attorney Suzannah Ryder's arsenal. His top secret activities, his suspicious confession and disappearance before the trial—nothing added up. With Justin refusing to be straight with her—for her protection, he claimed—could Suzannah prove him innocent as the evidence mounted against him?

#106 DARK REVELATIONS by Lorna Tedder
The Madonna Key

Trapped into becoming an antiquities thief for the powerful Adriano family, Aubrey De Lune had given up her daughter, her career, everything. But when she stole a sacred 600-year-old manuscript attributed to Joan of Arc, Aubrey discovered the Adrianos' dirty little secret…as well as the key to *her* heritage, *her* power…and getting her life back.

#107 GETAWAY GIRL by Michele Hauf

Getaway car driver Jamie MacAlister had finally "gotten away" from her dubious past working for a clandestine rescue force at odds with Paris law enforcement. Or had she? When clues to her former mentor's murder lured her back to the fast lane, the chase was on…but could Jamie put the brakes on her attraction to the prime suspect?

#108 TOO CLOSE TO HOME by Maureen Tan

By day she policed a small Illinois town. By night, she worked for the Underground, rescuing runaway women and children from abusive men. But Brooke Tyler's two worlds collided when she discovered the remains of a woman who'd died a decade ago, exposing secrets and unleashing a killer who would test her like never before….